BLOODY PASSAGE

JACK HIGGINS

OPEN ROAD

INTEGRATED MEDIA

NEW YORK

Published in 2010 by Open Road Integrated Media
180 Varick St.
New York, NY 10014
www.openroadmedia.com

For Hannah in some kind of Celebration

CONTENTS

CHAPTER ONE

A Season for Killing

THE FIRST SHOT RIPPED THE EPAULETTE from the right hand shoulder of my hunting jacket, the second lifted the thermos flask six feet into the air. The third kicked dirt at my right heel, but by then I was moving fast, diving headfirst into the safety of the reeds on the far side of the dike.

I surfaced in about four feet of stinking water, my feet sinking into the black mud of the bottom. The smell was really quite something—as if the whole world had rotted. I tried hard not to breathe too heavily as I crouched to get my bearings.

The marsh had come alive, mallard, wild duck and widgeon lifting out of the reeds in alarm, calling angrily to each other, and down by the shore beyond the sand dunes, several thousand flamingoes took off as one, filling the air with the pulsating of their wings. I waited, but there was no further word from my unknown admirer and after a while things quieted down.

The punctured thermos flask lay about three feet in front of my nose on the edge of the dike, dribbling coffee, but apart from that everything looked beautifully normal. The open picnic basket, the neat white cloth spread on the ground, salad, sandwiches, a rather large cold chicken, the bottle of wine I'd been about to open and Simone's easel with the water color she'd been working on, half finished.

Most interesting of all, and at that stage of things by far the most desirable item, the old Curtis Brown double-barreled sixteen-bore shotgun. It lay on the rug beside Simone's tin of water color paints, fifteen or twenty feet away, but as I'd only expected a crack at the odd duck or two it was hardly loaded for bear.

I gazed at it morosely, debating the possibility of a quick dash to retrieve it, carrying straight on into the reeds on the other side of the dike, but he was one jump ahead of me even on that point, although I suppose it was the logical move. I pushed the reeds to one side cautiously and started to ease forward and a bullet drilled a neat hole through the stock of the shotgun.

The .303 No. 4 Mark I Lee Enfield service rifle was the gun that got most British infantrymen through the Second World War. Recently resurrected by the British Army for use by its snipers in Ulster, it is a devastating weapon in the hands of a crack shot and accurate up to a thousand yards, which explains its popularity with the IRA also. Once heard in action, never forgotten and I'd heard a few in my time.

Certainly the specimen which was inflicting all the damage at that precise moment was in the hands of an expert. I pulled back into the reeds and waited because quite obviously the next move was his.

I found cigarettes and matches in the waterproofed breast pocket of my hunting jacket and lit up. It was perfectly still again. Even the flamingoes had returned to the shallows on the far side of the dunes. A flight of Brent geese drifted across the sky above me in a V formation, calling faintly, but the only other sound was the strange eerie whispering of the wind amongst the reeds.

Somewhere thunder rumbled uneasily at the edge of things which didn't surprise me for, in spite of the heat, the sky was grey and overcast and rain had threatened for most of the day.

About forty or fifty yards to my right on the same side of the dike there was a sudden crashing amongst the reeds and then a wild swan lifted into the air calling angrily. So, he was closer than I had imagined. A hell of a sight closer. I raised my head cautiously and became aware of the sound of an engine somewhere in the distance.

When I turned I could see the Landrover crossing the flooded causeway two hundred yards away, Simone at the wheel. She came up out of the water and drove along the top of the dike.

There wasn't much that I could do except put my head on the block like an officer and a gentleman, so I came up out of the reeds fast, grabbed for the shotgun and ran along the dike waving my arms at her, expecting a bullet between the shoulder blades at any moment.

It was really very interesting. One bullet kicked dirt to the left of me, another to the right. I was aware of Simone's face, wild-eyed in astonishment, and then as she braked to a halt, a third round drilled a hole through the windscreen to one side of her.

She stumbled out, white with fear. Another round thumped into the door panel behind her and I grabbed her hand and dragged her down over the edge of the dike into the cover of the reeds. She went in deep and surfaced, gasping for breath, her long dark hair plastered about her face. Another bullet slammed into the body of the Landrover.

She grabbed at the front of my jacket in blind panic. "What is it? What's happening?"

I took her hand, turned and pushed through the reeds until I was back in my original position. Another shot sliced through the reeds overhead and Simone ducked instinctively, going under again. She surfaced, her face streaked with filth and I took a couple of waterproof cartridges from one of my pockets and loaded the shotgun.

"He's good, isn't he?"

"For God's sake, Oliver," she said. "What is all this? Who's out there?"

"Now there you have me," I said. "He's a professional, I know that, but for the rest, it's really rather peculiar. You see, I have the distinct impression that he could have killed me any one of a dozen times and didn't. I wonder why?"

Her mouth opened in astonishment, the wide eyes above the high cheek-bones widened even more. She said in a hoarse voice. "You're actually enjoying this."

"Well it's certainly enlivened a rather dull afternoon, you must admit that."

Our friend fired again, shooting off the right hand leg of the easel so that it toppled over the dike into the water.

"Damn his eyes," I said. "I liked that painting. It was coming along fine. The way you were soaking the blues into the background wash was particularly pleasing."

She turned, her face contorted with fear, looking as if she might break into pieces at any moment. "Please, Oliver, do something! I can't take any more of this!"

The wine bottle exploded like a small bomb, showering glass everywhere, staining the white cloth scarlet.

"Now that really does annoy me," I said. "Lafite 1961. A really exceptional claret. I was going to surprise you. Here, hold this."

I gave her the shotgun and took off my hunting jacket. "What are you going to do?" she demanded.

I told her and when I'd finished, she seemed a little calmer, but was still obviously very frightened. I kissed her briefly on the cheek. "Can you handle it?"

She nodded slowly. "I think so."

I slipped the jacket over the muzzle of the shotgun and eased it up over the top of the reeds. There was an immediate shot and as the jacket was whipped away, I cried out in simulated agony.

I turned to Simone who waited, white-faced, waist-deep in that foul water. "Now!" I whispered.

She screamed out loud, scrambled up on to the dike, got to her feet and started the run toward the Landrover. He fired once, chipping a stone a couple of yards in front of her. It was all it took and she stopped dead, crying out in fear and stood there, waiting for the ax to fall. There was a movement in the reeds to my right and then boots crunched in the gravel of the dike top.

"What happened?" a voice called in French.

He moved past me toward her, a young, sallow-faced man with shoulder-length hair and a fringe beard. He wore a reefer jacket and rubber waders and carried the Lee Enfield at waist level.

The oldest trick in the book and he'd fallen for it.

I slipped up out of the reeds and moved in close. I don't know whether it was the expression on Simone's face or—more probably—the distinct double click as I cocked the shotgun, but in any event, he froze.

I said in French, "Now put it down very carefully like a good boy and clasp your hands behind your neck."

I knew he was going to shoot by the way his right shoulder started to lift, which was a pity because he didn't really leave me much choice.

He turned, crouching, to fire from the hip and Simone screamed. Having little choice in the matter I gave him both barrels in the face, lifting him off his feet and back over the edge of the dike into the reeds.

The marsh came alive again, birds rising out of the reeds in alarm, calling to each other, wheeling endlessly. Simone stood there transfixed, her face very white, staring down at the body. Most of him was submerged, only the legs from the knees to the feet encased in the rubber waders floated on the surface.

The next bit wasn't going to be pleasant, but it had to be done. I said, "I'd go back to the Landrover if I were you; this won't be nice."

Her voice was the merest whisper and she shook her head stubbornly. "I'd rather stay with you."

"Suit yourself."

I handed her the shotgun, got down on my hands and knees, secured a firm grip on each ankle and hauled him up on to the dike. Simone gave an involuntary gasp, and I didn't blame her when I saw his face, or what was left of it.

I said, more to get her out of the way than anything else, "Bring me the rug, there's a good girl."

She stumbled away and I opened the jacket and searched him, whistling softly between my teeth. It didn't take long, mainly because there was nothing to find. I squatted back on my heels and lit a cigarette and Simone returned. She still clutched the shotgun in one hand, the rug in the other which she handed me mutely.

As I wrapped it around his head and shoulders, I said, "Curiouser and curiouser, just like Alice. Empty pockets, no identity marks in the clothing." I lifted his hand. "Indentation in the left finger where a signet ring has habitually been worn, but no ring."

A professional all right. Stripped for action so that there would be no possibility of tracing him or his masters if anything went wrong. But I didn't say so to Simone because when I looked up, the dark eyes burned in the white face and her hands were shaking. She tightened her grip on the shotgun as if making an effort to hold herself together.

"Who was he, Oliver?"

"Now there you have me, angel."

"What did he want?" The anger in her was barely contained. It was as if she might blow up at any moment.

"I'm sorry," I said gently. "I can't help you. I'm as much in the dark as you."

"I don't believe you." The anger overflowed now, all the tension, the fear of the past ten or fifteen minutes pouring out of her. "You weren't afraid when you were out there, not for a single moment. You knew exactly what you were doing. It was as if that kind of thing was your business and you were too good. Too good with this!" She brandished the shotgun fiercely.

I said calmly, "It's a point of view, I'll give you that."

I knelt down beside the dead man, heaved him over my shoulder and stood up. She said quickly, "What are you going to do? Get the police?"

"The police?" I laughed out loud. "You've got to be joking."

I bent down and picked up his Lee Enfield then walked along the dike toward the Landrover. There was a patch of bog amongst the reeds on my right; black viscous mud. The sort of place that might be five feet deep or bottomless. When I tossed him in he slid beneath the surface instantly. There was a bubble or two, the stink of marsh gas. I threw the Lee Enfield after him and turned.

Simone was standing watching me, still clutching the shotgun, a kind of numbed horror on her face. Thunder rattled like distant drums again, overhead this time, and the rain which had threatened all day came with a rush, hissing into the reeds.

It was somehow symbolic, I suppose, for with a sudden fierce gesture Simone tossed the shotgun over my head, out into the reeds. She started to cry bitterly, shoulders shaking and I put my arms about her.

"It's all right," I said soothingly. "Everything's fine. I'll take you home now."

I turned and led her along the dike toward the Landrover.

I half-filled a tall glass with crushed ice, added a double measure of Irish gin and topped up with tonic water. Then I switched on the radio and turned the dial to Madrid. A little flamenco music would have been appropriate, but all I got was an old Glen Miller recording of *Night and Day*.

I pushed open one of the glass doors and moved out onto the terrace. Rain dripped from the fringes of the sun awning and I could smell the mimosa, heavy and clinging on the damp air.

The villa was built to a traditional Moorish pattern and stood in splendid isolation, which was the main reason I'd bought it, on a point of rock a hundred feet above a horseshoe cove thirty or forty miles southeast of Almeria toward Cape de Gata.

I'd been here almost a year now and never tired of the view, even on an evening like this with rain falling. There were lights outside the cove, not too far away, where local fishermen were stringing their nets and a liner drifted through the darkness five or six miles out and beyond it, Africa.

It all filled me with a vague, irrational excitement or perhaps it was just the events of the afternoon catching up. Heavy beads of rain rolled down the door and Simone became part of the room's reflection in the dark glass.

The black hair hung to her shoulders, she wore a plain linen caftan so long that it brushed her bare feet. It was an original, soaked in vegetable dyes in a back room in some Delhi bazaar until it had reached that exact and unique shade of scarlet so that it seemed to catch fire there in the half-shadows of the room.

I turned and toasted her. "You can cook, too. The meal was enormous."

She said gravely, "I'll get you another drink," and went behind the bar in the corner.

"That sounds like a good idea." I sat on one of the high cane stools and pushed my glass across.

She took down the gin bottle. "I didn't even know there was such a thing as Irish gin until I met you."

"As I remember, that was quite an evening."

"The understatement of this or any other year," she said lightly as she spooned ice into my glass.

Fair comment I'd met her at a party in Almeria thrown by some Italian producer who was making a Western or unreasonable facsimile, up in the Sierra Madre. I was strictly uninvited, pulled in by a scriptwriter I'd met in a waterfront bar, someone I knew barely well enough to exchange drinks with.

The party was a creepy sort of affair. Most of the men were middle-aged and for some reason found it necessary to wear sunglasses even at that time of night. The girls were mainly dolly birds, eager to comply with any and every demand that might lead along the golden path to stardom.

My scriptwriter friend left me alone and belligerent. I didn't like the atmosphere or the company and I was already half-cut, a dangerous combination. I pushed my way across to the bar which was being serviced by a young man with shoulder-length blond hair and a suit of purest white. His face looked vaguely familiar. The kind of cross between male and female that seems so popular these days. Anything from a manly aftershave advertisement to a second-rate movie and instantly forgettable.

"Gin and tonic," I said. "Irish."

"You've got to be joking, old stick," he said loudly in a phony English public school voice, and appealed to the half-dozen or so girls who were hanging on his every word at the end of the bar. "I mean, who ever heard of Irish gin?"

"It may not be in your vocabulary, sweetness," I told him, "but it certainly figures in mine."

There was what might be termed a rather frigid silence and he stopped smiling. A finger prodded me painfully in the shoulder and a hoarse American voice said, "Listen, friend, if Mr. Langley says there's no such thing as Irish gin, then there's no such thing."

I glanced over my shoulder. God knows where they'd found him. A latter-day Primo Carnera with a face that went with around fifty or so professional fights, too many of which had probably ended on the canvas.

"I bet you went over big, back there in Madison Square Gardens," I said. "Selling programs."

There was a second of shocked surprise, just long enough for the fact that I didn't give a damn to sink in, and then his fist came up.

A rather pleasant French voice said, "Oh, there you are, cheri. I've been looking everywhere for you."

A hand on my sleeve pulled me round. I was aware of the dark wide eyes above the cheekbones, the generous mouth. She smiled brightly and said to Langley, "I'm sorry, Justin. Can't let him out of my sight for a moment."

"That's okay, honey," Langley told her, but he wasn't smiling and neither was his large friend as she pushed me away through the crowd.

We fetched up in a quiet corner by the terrace. She reached for a glass from a tray carried by a passing waiter and put it into my hand.

"What were you trying to do, commit suicide? That was Mike Gatano you were arguing with back there. He was once heavyweight boxing champion of Italy."

"Christ, but they must have been having a bad year." I tried the drink she'd handed me. It burned all the way down. "What in the hell is this? Spanish whiskey? And who's the fruit, anyway?"

"Justin Langley. He's a film actor."

"Or something."

She leaned against the wall, arms folded, a slight frown on her face, a pleasing enough picture in a black silk dress, dark stockings and gold high-heeled shoes.

"You're just looking for it tonight, aren't you?"

"Gatano?" I shrugged. "All he is is big. What are you trying to do anyway, save my immortal soul?"

Her face went a little bleak, she started to turn away and I grabbed her arm. "All right, so I'm a pig. What's your name?"

"Simone Delmas."

"Oliver Grant." I reached for another glass as a waiter went past. "You want to know something, Simone Delmas? You're like a flower on the proverbial dung heap." I gestured around the room. "Don't tell me you're in the movies."

"Sometimes I do a little design work, just for the money. When I do what I prefer, I paint water colors."

"And who needs them in this world of today?"

"Exactly. It's really very sad. And you—what do you do?"

"Well, that's a matter of opinion. Write, I think. Yes, I suppose you could say I was a writer."

Langley's voice was raised behind as he moved into another public performance. "Surely we're all agreed that Vietnam was the most obscene episode of the century?"

I turned and found him in the center of an eager group of girls. They all nodded enthusiastically. He smiled, then noticed me watching. "Don't you agree, old stick?" he demanded and there was a challenge in his voice.

I was a fool to respond, I suppose, but the last two drinks were like fire in my belly. I didn't like him and I didn't like his friends and I wasn't too bothered about letting the whole world know.

"Well now," I said, "if you mean was it a dirty, stinking, rotten business, I agree, but then most wars are. On the other hand as a participant I tend to have rather personal views."

There was genuine shock on his face. "You mean you actually served in Vietnam?" he said. "My God, how dare you. How dare you come to my party."

I was aware of Gatano moving in behind me and Simone Delmas tugged at my sleeve. "Let's go!"

"Oh, no," Langley told her sharply. "He doesn't get off that easily. I know he didn't come with you, sweetie." He moved closer. "Who brought you?"

"Richard Burton," I said and kicked him under the right kneecap.

He went down hard, but without making much of a fuss about it which surprised me, but I had other things on my mind. Gatano grabbed my shoulder and I gave him a reverse elbow strike that must have splintered three of his ribs.

I wasn't too sure what happened after that. There was a great deal of noise and confusion and then I surfaced to find myself leaning against the wall in an alley at the side of the house. It was raining slightly and Simone was pulling my coat collar up about my neck.

"So there you are." She smiled. "Do you do this kind of thing often?"

"Only on Fridays," I said. "My religion forbids me to eat meat."

"Have you got a car?"

"A white Alfa. It should be around here somewhere."

"Where do you live?" I told her and she frowned. "That's forty miles away. You can't possibly drive that far in the state you're in."

"You could." I fished the keys from my pocket and held them out. "Nice night for a drive. You can stay over if you like. Plenty of room and bolts on all the bedroom doors."

I followed this up by starting to slide down the wall and she caught me quickly. "All right, you win, only don't pass out on me."

I leaned heavily on her all the way to the car and only passed out when she'd got me into the passenger seat.

When I woke up the following day it was almost noon and she was painting on the terrace using some old oil paints she'd found in a cupboard in the living room. It seemed she liked the view as much as I did. She was still there at sunset. And after that....

Two months —probably the happiest I'd known in years, I told myself as I sipped the drink she pushed across the bar to me.

"Is it all right?" she said.

"Perfect."

She folded her arms and leaned on the bar. "What do I know about you, Oliver? Really know?"

I raised my glass. "Well, for a start, I drink Irish gin."

"You write," she said, "or at least you once showed me a detective novel under another name and claimed it as yours."

"Come on, angel," I said. "If I'd been lying I'd have chosen something good."

"You have a scar on your right shoulder and another under the shoulder blade that suggests something went straight through."

"A birthmark," I said lightly. "Would you like me to describe yours? Strawberry and shaped like a primula. Back of the thigh just under the left buttock."

She carried straight on in the same calm, rather dead voice. "An American who could just as easily pass as an Englishman. A soldier because you did let slip at Justin's party that night in Almeria that you'd been in Vietnam, although you've never mentioned it since. An officer, I suppose."

"And gentleman?"

"Who can half kill a professional heavyweight boxer twice his size in two seconds flat."

"Poor old Gatano," I said. "He shouldn't have joined."

She seemed genuinely angry now. "Can't you ever be serious about anything?"

She moved to the end of the bar as if to put distance between us, took a cigarette from an ivory box and lit it with shaking fingers. She inhaled deeply once then stubbed it out in the ashtray.

There was a direct challenge now as she turned to confront me. "All right, Oliver. This afternoon. What was it all about?"

"I haven't the slightest idea," I told her with perfect truth.

For a moment I thought she might make a frontal assault. Instead she hammered on the bar with a clenched fist in fury. "I'm frightened, Oliver! Scared to death!"

I moved to take her hand. "No need to be, I promise you. Not as long as I'm here."

She gazed at me, eyes wide for a moment, then sighed, shaking her head slightly, and moved across to the window. She stood looking out into the night, arms folded in that inimitable way of hers, rain drifting across the terrace.

"Rain, rain, go to Spain, never come my way again," she said in a lost little-girl voice.

I moved in behind her and slid my arms around her waist. "Come to bed."

"Do you know what's the most frightening thing of all?" she said without looking round.

"No, tell me."

"That man out there in the marsh. He was a professional, you said so yourself, and yet he didn't stand a chance, did he?"

She half-turned, looking up at me. I kissed her gently on the mouth. "Come to bed," I said again and took her hand and led her out of the room.

I came awake from a dreamless sleep to find her gone. The windows to the terrace stood open and the white nylon curtains rose and fell in the gray light of dawn. I reached for my watch. Six-thirty.

I got out of bed, found a bathrobe and went into the living room. There was no sign of her there either, but somewhere a car door banged. I went out on the terrace and looked down to the drive.

The Alfa stood outside the garage. Simone was standing beside it dressed in slacks and sweater. A black leather suitcase was on the ground at her feet and she was stowing another behind the driver's seat.

"Good morning," I called cheerfully.

She looked up at me. Her face was very pale and there were faint shadows under each eye as if she had not slept too well.

She hesitated and for a moment I thought she was going to get into the car, but she didn't. Instead, she put the second suitcase inside and came toward the outside steps, her feet crunching in the gravel.

I returned to the living room, went behind the bar and poured myself a large gin and tonic. A bit early in the day, even for me, but I had a feeling I was going to need it.

She paused at the window, looking in. I raised my glass and smiled brightly. "Join me for breakfast?"

But she didn't smile. Not then or later. I don't think it was in her anymore.

"I'm sorry, Oliver," she said. "I'd hoped you wouldn't waken."

"What, not even a note?"

Her voice was full of pain, ragged and unsteady. "I can't take it—not any of it. What happened yesterday afternoon especially."

She shuddered visibly. I said, "Where are you going to go?"

"I don't know. It doesn't really matter. Paris maybe. Do you mind if I take the Alfa?"

I wasn't angry. There wouldn't have been any point. I said, "You were going to anyway."

"I'll leave it in Almeria. At the station."

"How are you for money?"

"I'll get by."

I dropped to one knee behind the bar and prised up one of the ceramic tiles. Underneath was a black tin cash box containing my mad money, just in case of emergencies. An old habit. I counted out ten one hundred-dollar bills and put them on top of the bar.

She didn't argue, simply walked across and picked them up. She looked around the room for a long moment and there was an infinite sadness in her voice when she said, "I was happy here. For the first time in years I was truly happy."

I said, "One thing before you go. That night after Langley's party when I passed out on you. Well, I didn't. I just wanted you to know that."

She said bitterly, "Damn you, Oliver! Damn you to hell!"

She walked out, her footsteps echoed across the terrace. I poured myself another large gin with a steady hand. From somewhere a thousand miles away a door slammed. There was a pause, the engine started and then she was gone.

So that was very much that. And why worry? As a great man once said, a woman was only a woman. I raised my glass and found that my hand was not so steady after all and that would never do. I put the glass down very deliberately on the bar top, went into my bedroom and found a pair of bathing shorts. Then I went out onto the end terrace and descended the three hundred and twenty-seven concrete steps which zigzagged down the cliff to the beach below.

The morning was dull and gray and the white sand cold to my feet as I crossed to the boathouse by the small stone jetty. I opened the door and went in. Skin-diving being closer to a religion with me than a sport at that time, I carried a pretty comprehensive range of equipment. Everything from my own compressor for recharging air bottles to an Aquamobile.

I took down a neoprene wetsuit in black and pulled it on because from the look of that sky it was going to be cold down there this morning. I slipped my arms through the straps of a fully charged aqualung, found a face mask and went back outside.

I had an inflatable with an outboard motor on the beach beside the jetty, but I didn't bother with it. Simply pulled on the mask, waded into the sea and struck out toward the entrance to the cove. I did this most mornings. So much so that it had become a habit, mainly because of the fascinating wreck I'd discovered about a hundred yards beyond the point.

There was a heavy sea mist rolling in toward me pushed by the wind and it started to rain again, not that that bothered me. There wasn't much of a current and it took little effort to reach the appropriate spot. I dropped under the surface, paused to adjust my air supply and went straight down.

Visibility was excellent in spite of the gray morning and the water was clear as glass. At fifty feet I entered a neutral zone, colors muted, a touch of autumn and then a ship's stern moved out of the gloom.

I hung onto a rail with some care for they were covered with black mussels and her plates were encrusted with dog's teeth, a razor-edged clam quite capable of opening you up like a gutting knife.

The name across the counter was clearly visible, *S.S. Finbar.* I'd checked up on her after that first discovery. A Clydeside freighter of three thousand tons. Strayed from a Malta convoy in the summer of 1942 and sunk by Stuka dive bombers.

She was tilted slightly to one side, her anti-aircraft gun still in place on the foredeck and remarkably well preserved. I moved toward it and paused, hanging on to the rail, adjusting my air supply again.

There was a sudden turbulence in the water and I glanced up and saw an Aquamobile descending, two divers hanging on behind. It drifted to a halt ten or fifteen feet above me. The divers were wearing bright orange wetsuits and black masks. One of them waved cheerfully, dived down and hung on to the rail beside me.

I leaned close, putting my mask close to his. The face seemed oddly familiar, which didn't make much sense and then he reached over and in one quick gesture ripped my air hose away from my mouth.

The whole thing was so unexpected that I took in water at once. I started to struggle, instinctively clawing for the surface and he moved fast, grabbing for my ankles, pulling me down.

I was going to die and for what, that was my final thought as everything started to go. And then I became aware of the other diver dropping down, towing a spare aqualung, holding its air hose out towards me, silver bubbles spiralling out of the mouthpiece. It seemed to grow very large, to completely envelope me, then I blacked out.

I surfaced to a world of pain, my head twisting from side to side as I was slapped into life like a newborn baby. I suppose I must have cried out because somewhere, someone laughed and a voice said, "He'll live."

I opened my eyes. I was lying in the bottom of an inflatable boat. Justin Langley was bending over me wearing an orange wetsuit, his long blond hair tied at the nape of his neck in a kind of eighteenth-century queue. Gatano, in a similar suit, worked the outboard motor.

Langley smiled. "You don't look too good, old stick."

I tried to sit up and he pushed me down without the slightest effort. At the same moment his friend called, "We're here," and cut the engine.

A Cessna seaplane drifted toward us through the mist, we slid in under the port wing and bumped against a float. I tried to sit up and Langley shoved me down again. There was a hypodermic in his right hand now and he smiled.

"Go to sleep like a good boy and we'll try to see you don't get airsick."

Whatever it was, it was good. I felt the needle going in, but he probably enjoyed that part. And then, total darkness. A split second in time that must have been in reality five or six hours before I returned to life again.

It was cold and damp and very dark. I was walking, supported on either side, descending some steps that seemed to go on forever. When we finally stopped, there was only a narrow circle of light. I was aware of Langley's face looming very large, serious now and two men on their knees levering a round iron grid out of the floor. It was very dark down there and quiet.

Langley slapped my face. It didn't hurt at all. He said, "Still with us?" And then he turned and nodded to the others. "Down he goes."

I didn't attempt to struggle, I was incapable of that. A rope or a strap of some sort was looped around me and I was lowered perhaps ten or fifteen feet into darkness. There was a clang as the iron grid was replaced, footsteps echoed away.

I became aware of two things almost in the same instant. That I was only wearing the bathing shorts I had put on that morning and that when I stretched out my arms on either side, I immediately touched damp stone walls.

Not that it mattered, not then, for as yet, nothing touched me. I slumped down in a corner, knees to my chest in the fetal position and drifted back into my drugged sleep.

CHAPTER TWO

THE HOLE

IT WAS THE COLD WHICH BROUGHT me awake more than anything else and I crouched there in the dark corner, trying to get my bearings. A ray of sunlight drifted out of a channel in the stonework high above my head. I squinted up at it, tried to get to my feet and lost my balance for the excellent reason that I was wearing leg irons and the foot of steel chain between my ankles restricted movement more than a little.

I lay there in the darkness thinking about it for a while, considering the possibility that the whole thing was simply a particularly vivid nightmare, when the iron grating at the top of the shaft was removed and Justin Langley peered in.

Gatano's battered face appeared at his right shoulder, something which at that stage of the game didn't surprise me in the least. He laughed hoarsely. "He don't look so good to me, Mr. Langley."

"A good hot meal inside you, that's what you need, old stick," Langley called. "Try this for size."

He lowered a large biscuit tin on a length of string. It contained a bottle of water and a plate of some kind of cold stew that smelled like a newly opened tin of inferior dog food.

I crouched there like some dumb animal, helpless with rage. Gatano called, "Hey, you down there."

When I looked up he was urinating into the hole. I tried to toss the plate up in his general direction, a futile gesture as I got most of the dogmeat back on my own head.

Langley chuckled. "You'll change your mind, old stick. Tomorrow or the next day or the day after that, you'll eat it. I promise you."

My voice, when I answered him, was so calm, so much outside myself that I hardly recognized it as my own. "All right," I said. "What's it all about?"

The iron grid clanged into place shutting out all light and I sank down into the corner. *Some sort of complicated revenge for that evening in Almeria?* But that didn't make any kind of sense. The divers, the seaplane, this place. It was all too elaborate. There was some hidden meaning here, a deeper purpose and I drifted into sleep again thinking about it.

Most men spend their lives trying to claw their way out of one kind of a hole or another, but mine was something very special indeed. A stone shaft fifteen feet deep and four feet square and unclimbable, especially in those leg irons. It was only possible to lie down corner-to-corner, but it was so damn cold that I usually preferred to curl up in as tight a ball as possible.

No blankets and definitely no sanitary arrangements so that by the third day, the stench in that confined space had to be experienced to be believed. I could mark the passage of time simply enough by the light which filtered in through the narrow channel in the stonework above my head and there was always the daily ration lowered in the biscuit tin, although after that first day, it was never possible to see who was up there. I tried calling a few times, but nobody ever answered, and after a while I gave up, for it was obviously the intention to isolate me from any kind of human contact.

It was always the same—a bottle of water and the dog food and Langley was right. By the third day I was cleaning the plate, but boredom was the main problem. There was always sleep, but the cold didn't help too much there so I tried passing the time by undertaking a kind of personal psychoanalysis.

Freud would have been proud of me. I actually made it back to my third birthday; for the first time since that happy event recalled burying a box of scarlet-coated Grenadier Guards in a cornfield at the back of my English grandfather's Dorset farmhouse and the feeling of utter desolation at forgetting where. And the next day my father, who was a captain in the Marine Corps stationed at the American Embassy in London …

The grating clanged above my head and Langley peered in. I got to my feet and looked up at him. By my reckoning it was exactly a week since that first morning.

"My God," he said. "Something must have crawled in and died. Hose him down."

The jet of water which followed was cold, but really quite pleasant. It stopped after a while and Langley leaned over and lowered a rope with a loop on the end.

"All right," he said. "Up with you."

I came up out of the darkness and found myself in some sort of vault, stone pillars supporting the roof. It was neatly whitewashed and lit by electric light and stone steps in one corner led up to a stout oak door. Two men had the other end of the rope, peas out of the same pod, dark, swarthy looking, wearing identical heavy fishermen's sweaters, capable of most things if appearances were anything to go by.

They released the rope and one of them said to the other in Italian, "Mother of God, he stinks like a dung heap."

Justin Langley came forward, Gatano at his back. His blond hair hung to his shoulders. He wore a black nylon shirt, skin tight and open at the neck. The broad belt at his waist had a round brass buckle that must have been four inches in diameter and he wore a gold chain round his neck with a bauble on the end which he twirled between his fingers.

I said, "You look sweet—honestly."

"I wish you wouldn't, old stick." He sighed. "It brings out the worst in me."

He nodded to Gatano who moved forward, a look of what might be termed eager anticipation on his face. When he was close enough he put a fist into my belly. As I doubled over, he hooked his foot under the chain between my ankles and pulled me down.

Langley said sharply, "Don't mark his face!"

I wasn't sure whether Gatano had heard him or not for he was obviously enjoying himself. He put his boot into me, not very scientifically, three or four times, grunting with effort and then Langley said, "All right, that's enough!" and pulled him off.

They put the hose on me again and the two Italians picked me up between them and we followed Langley and Gatano up the stone steps. Gatano opened the door and we went out into bright morning sunshine.

I was beginning to function again, well below par, but enough to get by for the moment. We had emerged into a cobbled courtyard surrounded by stone walls. There was a gate at the far end and on the right, steps up to ramparts.

I negotiated them with some difficulty because of the leg irons, but the view was worth it. Massive cliffs, a calm blue sea shimmering in the heat haze, and above us at an even higher level, a citadel standing in a garden.

There was the scent of wisteria and I could smell almond trees as we passed through an iron gate into a semitropical paradise. There was the sound of water everywhere, splashing in fountains, gurgling in the conduits as it dropped from terrace to terrace between the palm trees.

We climbed a final flight of steps and emerged on to a broad terrace at a point where the ramparts came together like the prow of a ship. The view was really quite astonishing. There was a table beneath an awning, white linen cloth, silverware, a couple of bottles of wine in a bucket, a waiter in a neatly starched coat at the ready, napkin folded over one arm.

His master stood at the ramparts, an immensely fat man in a white linen suit, long, dark hair flecked with silver. When he turned I saw that he had a walking stick in each hand and leaned heavily on both of them.

It was a strange face, dark, hooded eyes that seemed to look through and beyond you. A brutal, rather sensual mouth and overall a kind of total arrogance. And it was a familiar face, that was the most disturbing thing of all, yet for the life of me I couldn't remember where I'd seen him before.

He examined me for a long moment, those strange, brooding eyes giving nothing away, then he shuffled across to the table and eased himself down into a wicker chair. He nodded to the waiter who took one of the bottles from the bucket and filled a glass. I was immediately aware of the distinctive aroma of *anis*.

"Your health, Major Grant," he toasted me.

He had a deep bass voice, totally American, nothing of Europe in it at all. I said, "You want to watch it. Too much of that stuff in the heat of the day can freeze your liver. I've seen it put strong men on their backs for a week."

Langley started to say something, but my fat friend waved him down with one hand. He stared at me intently, a frown on his face, then smiled. "By God, you know where you are, sir. Confess it!"

"I think so."

He slapped his thigh in high good humor and turned to Langley. "Didn't I tell you I'd picked the right man?"

Langley twirled the golden bauble between his fingers. "He has a big mouth, I'll give you that."

The fat man turned his attention back to me and leaned forward, hands folded over the handle of one of his walking sticks. "Come, sir, don't let me down."

"All right." I shrugged. "The architecture of this fortress for a start. Walls are Norman, probably twelfth century. Most of the rest is Moorish. Then there's the garden. Papyrus by the main pool, another Arab innovation, and the wine you're drinking. *Zibibbo* from the island of Pantellaria. I can smell the *anis.*"

"Which all adds up to?"

"Sicily." I squinted up at the sun. "Somewhere on the southern coast."

"Southeast," he said. "Capo Passero to be exact." He shook his head solemnly, sipped a little of his wine and said to Langley, "Remarkable is it not, what the trained mind is capable of?"

Langley looked sullen, picked up a wineglass and held it out to the waiter who filled it for him. The fat man chuckled. "Justin is not impressed, Major Grant, but then he likes to be first in the field always. It comes of having been educated at Eton."

"You mean the reformatory?" I said. "In Northern Nebraska?" I shook my head. "Poor kid, I don't suppose he ever really stood a chance."

Strangely enough Langley reacted to that one with apparent indifference, but his fat friend rocked with laughter. "I like that. Yes, I really like that." He wiped tears from his eyes with a large white pocket handkerchief. "You know who I am, Major Grant?"

"I don't think so."

"Stavrou, sir. Dimitri Stavrou." He expected a reaction and seeing it in my face, grinned slyly. "You know me now, I think?"

"I should," I said. "Your picture was on enough front pages nine or ten months ago when they deported you from the States."

"An affront to justice." He seemed angry for the moment, though whether this was genuine or assumed, it was impossible to say. "Although I was born in Cyprus, I lived in America for forty years of my life, Major Grant. I had legitimate business interests."

"Like gambling, drugs, prostitution?" I said. "Front man for the Syndicate or the Mafia or whatever they call themselves these days, wasn't that it?"

There was a hot spark of anger behind those dark eyes. "The pot, sir, calling the kettle black, isn't that how the English would put it?" He snapped his fingers. "The file, Justin, there's a good boy."

There was a briefcase leaning against the back of Stavrou's cane chair. Langley opened it, took out a buff colored folder and laid it on the table in front of him.

Stavrou put a hand on it. "Oliver Berkley Grant. In detail."

"What, warts and all?" I said.

"I must know it by heart by now." He pushed it away ostentatiously and closed his eyes. "Father, colonel in the Marine Corps, killed in action in Korea in 1951. Mother English. You were educated at an English public school, Winchester. That was to please her, then West Point. You first went to war the year your father was killed. By the end of the Korean conflict you had collected a D.S.C. and Silver Star and a wound which put you in hospital for nine months. It was the last time you fought in any conventional sense as a soldier."

Most of this had been delivered in a rather flat monotone at some speed and now, he opened his eyes. "How am I doing?"

"Now I know where I've seen you before," I said. "Gypsy Rose. You had a tent two summers ago on the boardwalk at Atlantic City."

He was not provoked in the slightest. "For the next seven years, Special Services Executive, Major Grant. Military Intelligence. You became especially expert at getting people out of places. After the Bay of Pigs fiasco the Cubans got their hands on an American colonel named Hurwitz. They intended to stage a show trial that would expose America to the world and then on the night of..." He hesitated. "The 31st October, am I right? You landed with half a dozen special service troops and spirited Hurwitz away from an apparently impregnable fortress."

I was shaken now, rocked straight back on my heel, because what he was giving out was classified information at the highest level.

"You must be on good terms with the President."

"A brilliant operation which made you famous in the Pentagon, at least in a discreet way and one you repeated seven or eight times over the ensuing years. Cuba once again. Cambodia, twice in Vietnam and then Albania. An American U2 pilot named Murphy was to be put on trial as a spy. You got him out of the top state security prison in Tirana."

"It's just a knack," I said. "Something my old grannie taught me when I was in short pants."

"And now we come to August, 1966," he said. "Sylvia Gray, a seventeen-year-old student from Boston, daughter of a friend of your grandfather. An impulsive young lady who went to Prague with a group of other students during the Czechoslovakian revolt and was sentenced to life imprisonment for the murder of a Russian soldier. She shot him in the back three times."

"That's right," I said. "He was trying to rape a fourteen-year-old girl at the time."

"You went to your superiors and asked permission to get the girl out and they refused."

Strange that I could feel the same impotent rage so many years later.

"So you went anyway, entered Czechoslovakia illegally and with the help of an underground organization broke the girl out of jail and got her safely home after a rather public gun fight on the Austria-Czech border."

"You seem to know it all."

"But I do. Everything. A General Court Martial, all highly secret, but just as nasty. They stripped you bare and dumped you in disgrace, well and truly on your ass, if you'll excuse such an uncouth expression."

And now I was worried because he really had got too close for comfort and I waited for the axe to fall.

"Which left you in one hell of a fix because you had responsibilities. The year your father was killed, your mother died in childbirth leaving a little girl, your sister, Hannah. Twenty years your junior. A grave responsibility. Your maternal grandmother raised her in London. You provided for both of them. More than essential in view of the fact that your sister is totally blind, but then, her musical gifts make up for that to some extent. She studies piano at the Royal College of Music, I understand."

"All right," I said. "It's been fun, really it has, only let's get to the point."

"You tried writing thrillers, which brought you only a modest return, and then you were approached in London by an ex-British Intelligence officer who knew something of your background. There was a man in prison in Birmingham, one of a number who had robbed a train of several million pounds, most of which had never been recovered. With only a thirty-year sentence to look forward to, he was happy to pay fifty thousand pounds into a Swiss bank account to anyone who could get him out and you couldn't resist the challenge, could you, Major Grant?"

"I wish you wouldn't keep calling me that," I said. "Under the circumstances it's almost obscene."

"After that, you never looked back. A reasonably constant demand for the services of someone with your very special talents. When you retired last year you had over four hundred thousand pounds in your Geneva account. Would you like the number, by the way?"

There was a longish pause as if he actually expected an answer. I glanced at Langley who smiled beautifully. "You're really quite a card, aren't you, old stick?"

"So there you were," Stavrou said, "with all the money in the world, or so it seemed, so that when someone approached you three months ago and offered you one hundred thousand dollars to get a young American named Stephen

Wyatt out of a penal colony in Libya where he was recently sentenced to life imprisonment, you refused."

There was a long pause and then the whole thing suddenly clicked into place. "You?" I said.

"Stephen Wyatt is my stepson, Major Grant," he told me softly. "My dead wife's son. A stupid, misguided boy who dropped out of Yale after war service with the Paratroops in Vietnam, came out to the Mediterranean and got mixed up with some counter revolutionary organization in Libya aimed at overthrowing Colonel Quadhafi."

"And they gave him life?" I said.

"Exactly. I want him out."

My anger was like a fuse slow-burning. I said, "Are you telling me this whole thing was a set-up from the beginning? The guy in the marsh at Cape de Gata with his Lee Enfield, for instance?"

"Now he did get a little over enthusiastic," Stavrou said. "All he was supposed to do was rattle you. Leave you a little worried, but he went too far."

"And bit off more than he could chew."

"An impressive performance, major, I must say. He was actually supposed to be resting, isn't that the term theatricals use? A young man who'd had a considerable success as a sniper in Ulster with the Provisional IRA."

"And everything since? The Hole, for example?"

"You're surely familiar with brainwashing techniques, particularly as practiced by the Chinese? Pavlovian in concept. First of all it is necessary to bring about the complete alienation of the individual, destroy his confidence in any kind of order or pattern to his life. Degrade him if at all possible."

Langley said, with a grin, "We certainly did a good job of that, old stick, credit where credit's due."

I gave him some old-fashioned Anglo Saxon, tried to reach him and tripped over my chains. Stavrou said, "I wished to show you that I hold you in the hollow of my hand, my friend. That was the sole purpose of the exercise. There is nowhere you can run. Nowhere you can be certain of safety. No single person you can trust."

"You go to hell," I said.

He smiled patiently. "I'll prove it to you. The final and ultimate truth." He reached for a small handbell and rang it.

A moment later, Simone Delmas came through a gate in the wall and stood beside him, a hand on his shoulder, her face calm, untroubled. She wore a silk mini dress in olive green open at the throat.

"Is she not lovely, Major Grant?"

She leaned down to kiss him, he slipped a hand under the edge of the skirt, stroking her thigh, and opened the file.

"August 10th, Subject returned from Almeria with Miss Delmas at ten-thirty. They made love on the terrace. Four-thirty, subject returned from swimming with Miss Delmas. They made love on the terrace. Do you want me to go on? We do have some rather excellent film also." He smiled up at Simone, his hand steadily stroking the thigh. "She does enjoy this kind of thing so."

By then, of course, nothing was even halfway funny anymore. I said, "You're wasting your time. I won't play."

"Oh, but I think you will." He levered himself to his feet. "If you'll be kind enough to follow me, I'll show you why."

It was going to be good, it had to be and I shuffled after him, giving Simone a wide berth, and they all followed. We passed through the garden to the far end. Someone somewhere was playing the piano, a piece I recognized for once, *April* from a little suite by Tchaikowsky called *The Seasons*. My throat went dry and I think I was already ahead of him as we paused by the barred window in the end wall.

"Your sister, Major Grant," he said calmly, "who you imagine to be in London at this very moment pursuing her studies. Take a look inside."

And she was there, of course, as I had known she must be, sitting at a grand piano in the center of what was obviously the library.

She was a small, quiet girl with a generous mouth, high cheekbones, black hair parted in the center and tied back tightly. Only a slightly vacant look in the dark eyes hinted at her condition.

I didn't see her very often, mainly because I had a vague superstitious feeling that in some way she might be tainted by what I had become. By the life I led, and I loved her too much for that. I'd contented myself over the years by providing for her every need and leaving her to my grandmother's care, safe and secure in her own small world in the house in St. John's Wood.

I'd last seen her at the Festival Hall in London nine months previously playing the final movement of Rachmaninoff's Third Piano Concerto in a Royal College of Music student's concert. There was the same look of total concentration on her face now.

The far door opened and a woman entered, a black and tan Doberman at her side. The animal crossed to Hannah, who stopped playing for a moment to fondle it.

"Amazing," Stavrou said. "Usually Frau Kubel is the only one who can even get near the beast."

Langley said, "His favorite trick is pulling people's arms off. I'd advise you to remember that, old stick."

Frau Kubel looked about sixty with a grim, bleak face, hair drawn back tightly into a bun. She wore a black bombazine dress and white apron and her legs were slightly bowed. If she'd ever been in a concentration camp it could only have been as a guard.

She said something to Hannah who stood up. Frau Kubel took her arm and they walked to the door and went out.

I said slowly, "How did you get her here?"

"She's supposed to be spending a holiday with you. It was easy enough to arrange. A phone call to your grandmother with a message from you. She saw the girl off at Heathrow and when she landed at Palermo yesterday, Justin at his most charming was there to greet her with a tale of your having been delayed." He smiled gravely. "You get the picture now, sir?"

The anger, the black, killing rage rose inside me like a living thing, but I fought to control it. "I think so."

"So long as we understand each other. From those ramparts down to the beach is all of four hundred feet. A long way to fall." He put a cigar in his mouth and Langley lit it for him. "Yes, a dangerous place." He blew out smoke in a long column. "Especially for someone with your sister's difficulties."

I tried to get at him, tripped over those damned chains and found myself on my hands and knees in front of him again. By some small miracle, Langley had an automatic in his right hand and screwed the muzzle into the side of my neck.

Stavrou gazed down at me dispassionately and I was aware of Simone standing behind him, hands on the back of the wheelchair, face wiped clean of all expression.

Stavrou said slowly, "All right, Grant, you were right. I've been in the rackets all my life. Al Capone, O'Bannion, Frank Nitti, Legs Diamond. I knew them all, only they're long gone and I'm still here. You know why? Because when I say it, I mean it. I always carry it through, no matter how rough."

He stopped talking for a moment and it was very quiet and then he continued, "My wife, Major Grant, was a lady, and I mean a lady. Boston Society and all that kind of stuff. When she said she'd marry me, I couldn't believe it. And the years we had together...."

He ran a hand wearily over his face. "This son of hers was always trouble, but before she died I promised her I'd see him through." He sighed, a brief ironic smile on his mouth. "I'm going to tell you something. That kid hates my guts, but it doesn't matter a damn. I'm going to get him out of that place for her sake, and you're going to see to it for me. Understand?"

To which there was little I could say—for the moment. He swung the wheel-chair round in a circle and said to Langley, "All right, bring him along."

Gatano pulled me to my feet, the two characters in the fisherman sweaters got an arm each and we all went back through the garden to the terrace. Someone positioned him at the table and filled a glass with more wine.

He sipped a little and looked up at me. "I'll make the point again. If you even attempt to step out of line, your sister takes a fall. You understand me?"

"Perfectly."

"Good." He nodded to Gatano. "Unchain him."

Gatano did as he was told without a word. I stood there flexing my wrists, feeling curiously unsteady. "What happens now?"

"That's up to you. You can have anything you want. Money, equipment, men. Just ask. As for this place where they're holding the boy—plans, maps, every scrap of information we could get hold of—you'll find all that in your room. And a man called Zingari is waiting to see you."

"Who's he?"

"There's a little town on the coast about fifteen miles from the prison called Zabia. He runs a bar there."

"Amongst other things?"

"Exactly. He should be more than useful."

I moved to the table, helped myself to a glass and one of the bottles of *Zibibbo*. It tasted fresh and cool, and as I drank it I noticed Simone's nose wrinkle in disgust, and she backed away slightly.

"I know, angel," I said. "I smell like a sewer. Isn't life hell?" She flushed angrily and I turned to Stavrou. "How long have I got?"

"Two weeks."

"And I've got a free hand?"

He nodded gravely. "Completely."

"To choose my own team?"

There was a moment of silence and Langley poured himself a glass of wine, a slight, cynical smile on his face.

Stavrou nodded to the two stalwarts in the fisherman sweaters. "Moro and Bonetti here are good men, and Justin ..."

"Always likes to be number one." I shook my head. "I wouldn't touch any of them with a ten-foot pole. My own team, or it's not on."

He laughed harshly and slapped his thigh. "I like a man who knows what he wants and goes after it. We'll play it your way."

"Good," I said. "And now if somebody would show me to my room I'd like a bath."

"Of course," Stavrou said. "But before you go there are a couple of rather important items to take care of." He looked up at Langley. "Check if the London call has come through yet."

Langley picked up the phone and spoke briefly in fluent Italian. He said to Stavrou, "The old lady's out, but they have the housekeeper on the line."

He held the phone out to me and Stavrou said, "You can always leave a message, Major Grant. We wouldn't want your grandmother to worry, now would we?"

I did as I was told, choking back the anger, then slammed the receiver back into place. "Can I go now?"

"Not yet." Stavrou nodded to Langley who picked up the phone again and pressed one of the intercom buttons. "Your sister, Major Grant. We don't want her to worry unnecessarily either, do we? You're in Cairo, I think. Delayed by important business. You hope to be with her in a matter of days."

Everyone watched as Langley held out the phone to me again. "I'd do as he says if I were you, old stick," he told me. "He can be a bit of a sod when he wants to be."

I could hear her voice, a faint echo as I reached for the receiver and forced myself to sound cheerful.

"Hannah? This is Oliver."

The delight in her voice was almost more than I could take in the circumstances and keeping that conversation going with Stavrou and his friends listening in politely was one of the hardest things I've ever had to do in my life.

When I finally put the phone down, my hand trembled slightly, the violence barely contained. "Can I go now?" I said hoarsely.

"But of course."

I turned and Gatano grabbed my shoulder. "Come on, you heard Mr. Stavrou. Move it."

Which was definitely the very last straw, so I pivoted, putting a knee into his fat gut, giving it to him again full in the face as he keeled over. He rolled down the steps into the bushes and when I swung to face him, Langley jumped back, hands raised defensively, something close to amusement on his face.

"Oh, no," I said. "Not today. I'm saving you until later, you bastard," and I turned and staggered down the steps into the garden, suddenly very tired.

CHAPTER THREE

THE HIGH TERRACE

THE BATHROOM WAS A TRIFLE TOO baroque for my taste. Water gushed from a golden lion's mouth into a black marble tub—that sort of thing, but it was good and hot and there was plenty of it. I lay there for an hour or more, soaking away the stink of the Hole and thinking about things.

My immediate impulse was to try and get Hannah out of there by any means possible, but that was easier said than done. Stavrou had granted me an apparent freedom of movement, but what that meant in actuality was something else again.

By the time I'd shaved, I was beginning to feel almost human. I put on a robe and went into the bedroom, towelling my hair. There was a Sicilian peasant woman in a crisp white overall laying clothes out on the bed who actually curtseyed on the way out.

Underwear, slacks, shirt, shoes—everything fitted perfectly which was impressive enough until I remembered Simone. Such minor details must have been easy enough for her to provide. I thought of her briefly as I dressed and with some bitterness, but only for a moment. There were, after all, more important things to think about.

When I went out on the terrace, there was a drinks trolley that even included a couple of bottles of Irish gin. Stavrou, or Simone, obviously thought of everything. Even more interesting was the fat manilla folder on the ironwork table, so I sat down and started to explore the contents with the aid of a large gin and tonic.

The prison itself was at a place called Râs Kanai and had quite a history. The Italians had built it originally as a military fortress in colonial times. During the war the Germans had had it and then the British. Since independence, the place appeared to have been well stocked with opponents of the government of Colonel Quadhafi or those who were suspected of falling into that category.

I was halfway through when the outer door of the bedroom opened and Langley appeared followed by a small man in a shabby white-linen suit. He had tiny anxious eyes, a pale, translucent skin that seemed perpetually damp and the merest whisper of a moustache.

Langley said, "And this little worm is one Benito Zingari, who may or may not be of use to you."

Zingari bobbed his head, fingering an old straw hat nervously in both hands. Langley said, "Ah, well, if nobody's going to offer me a drink, I'd better try elsewhere."

"Why don't you do just that?"

He smiled amicably and went out. I lit a cigarette and looked Zingari over. He smiled nervously and started to sweat.

I said, "They tell me you run a bar in Zabia."

"That's right, signor." His English was really very good indeed.

"What else do you do?"

"A little of this—a little of that." He shrugged. "A man must make out the best way he can."

"Cigarette smuggling?" I said. "Heroin? Women?"

He didn't reply, but there was an edge to him and a kind of cunning in his eyes. It was as if we understood each other and that fact in itself gave him confidence.

"All right," I said. "Help yourself to a drink and let's talk. Have you read this file?"

"I don't need to, signor."

"Okay, tell me about it."

"The prison is about fifteen miles away from Zabia, signor, on the coast high above the cliffs. Râs Kanai, they call it. Cape of Fear. It was originally an Italian fortress."

"Yes, I know all that," I said impatiently. "How many prisoners does it hold?"

"Five hundred."

"And guards?"

"Since Quadhafi's time it has been guarded by the military. Usually around six hundred troops under the command of Colonel Masmoudi." He shook his head. "A very bad man, signor. He has been known to beat prisoners to death personally."

I thought about it for a while and it didn't look good. The ratio of guards to prisoners, for example, was better than one for one, which was incredible.

"You're sure of those figures?"

He nodded. "A great many political offenders, signor. Some of them are very important people or were. Security is most strict. Colonel Masmoudi is a fanatical supporter of the Quadhafi regime. He would execute every prisoner in the place if ordered to."

Something else which didn't make the overall situation look any brighter. I said, "Stavrou's stepson, this Stephen Wyatt. He's twenty years old and they've given him life. What are his chances?"

"The average time served by those sentenced to life is three years, signor, because at the end of that time they are usually dead. They spend most of their time working in the chain gang in the salt marsh and Masmoudi allows no rest during the beat of the day. Men die like flies."

There was a plan of the fort in the folder and a map of the surrounding area. I unfolded them on the floor and we started to go over them. The walls on the land side were forty feet high, well protected by floodlighting and heavily guarded. On the side facing the sea, the fortifications were much simpler, the cliffs being a hundred and fifty feet high at that point and quite unclimbable, or so Zingari insisted.

"You're certain of this?" I asked him.

"Oh, yes, signor, I have been inside many times on business. I supply the officers' mess with wine and spirits."

I frowned. "Aren't they all Muslims? Isn't alcohol forbidden?"

"Not at Râs Kanai. Not since Masmoudi turned Communist and has ceased to practice his religion."

Which was interesting. Supplies were brought in by a military train, another relic of Italian Imperialism.

I said, "Does this thing unload inside the fortress?"

He nodded. "Oh, yes, signor, but believe me, there is no hope there. The train is searched most thoroughly with the aid of dogs each time it enters. In any event, it only carries military personnel or new prisoners."

I frowned down at the plan. "Doesn't anyone other than the military get into the damned place? Aren't there any civilian workers?"

"The military handle everything, signor," he said firmly and then pulled up short as if at a sudden thought and chuckled. "Of course, there are the women, signor. The Friday-night women. I was forgetting those."

"And which women would those be?"

"Another innovation of Colonel Masmoudi's. He's fond of the ladies and reasonable enough to realize that plenty of his men are in the same boat, so every Friday night they bring in a couple of truckloads of women from Zabia."

"Whores?"

"But of course, signor." He looked bewildered. "They must, after all, be capable of serving more than one man. It requires very special talents."

"I bet it does," I said. "And who supplies these ladies?"

He contrived to look suitably modest. "Why, I do, signor, and it is no easy matter, I can tell you. After a month or two a change is looked for. I have to bring girls from as far away as Tripoli."

"And the trucks?" I said. "Are they allowed in?"

"Oh, no, signor." He shook his head. "The women have to dismount outside and are checked in through the gate."

I sat there for two or three minutes, staring into space and he waited patiently. After a while he said, "Is there anything else, signor?"

I shook my head. "If I need you again, I'll send for you."

He moved to the french window and hesitated. "I have been of help, signor?"

"Oh, yes," I said. "I think you could say that."

He went out quietly and I lay back, eyes closed, going over it all in my mind and after a while, I dozed.

When I awakened it was evening and just before dusk. It was heavy and oppressive, a hint of rain in the air. I crossed the terrace and took the steps down into the garden. Palms swayed in the slight wind, their branches dark feathers against the evening sky that already showed a star here and there.

I moved on, taking a flight of steps up to the ramparts and found Simone leaning over the wall, staring down at the sea, outlined against a sky the color of brass. Perhaps she'd noticed me out of the corner of her eye down there in the garden as I approached, but she certainly gave no sign.

I lit a cigarette and flicked the match far out into the darkness. "Well?"

"Well what?" she said. "If you think I'm going to apologize, you've come to the wrong shop."

"No apologies needed," I said. "But a few facts would be appreciated."

"Such as?"

"Why you did it would do for starters."

"All right, Oliver." She turned to face me. "It was a job, that's all. Just another assignment."

"Well, you're a great little actress. I'll say that for you. You were particularly good at simulating orgasms, by the way. I'll be happy to give you a reference to that effect any time."

She struck out at me furiously, but I got a hand up to block the blow. "Damn you!" she said. "And just how honest were you with me, anyway?"

"A fair point," I said. "Strangely enough I can forgive you nearly all of it, but not Hannah. Never that. That was unforgivable and that was one side of me you did know about. One side of me I never hid from you."

Which hit home rather satisfactorily. Her shoulders sagged a little and she turned away to look out to sea. "Why Stavrou, for God's sake?" I said.

"Because I owe him," she replied. "Because he's been good to me. About three years ago I was in love with a man in Paris who trafficked in heroin. I didn't know it at the time, but when the police moved in, they were going to pull me down with him. I could have got ten years."

"And Stavrou saved your hide?"

"That's about it"

"Oh, I see it now," I said. "We've all misjudged him. Presumably he's like the toad in the fairy story. One kiss from your delicious lips and he'll change into a handsome young prince. Now that I can't wait to see."

She turned away angrily and we were suddenly hailed by Stavrou. "Over here, you two."

He was on the high terrace and as we went up the steps, someone switched on floodlighting. The table was laid for three only and Stavrou sat at the far end, the waiter standing behind him.

"Come and join me," he said jovially.

I pulled out a chair, Simone hesitated briefly, then sat down. The waiter doled out a local soup made with goat's cheese and served ice-cold. There was champagne to help things along.

"And where's friend Langley tonight?" I inquired.

"Entertaining your sister, naturally," Stavrou shrugged. "After all, one must keep the pretense up." I stiffened, which is putting it mildly, and he added good humoredly, "No need to fret, I assure you, sir. The idea of any young woman being in danger where Justin is concerned is really quite amusing."

Which was something, and I continued with the meal with as good a grace as possible under the circumstances. It was excellent and he obviously had a first rate local chef. We had *narbe di San Paolo,* which is ravioli filled with sugar and cheese and fried, and *cannolo* to follow and more champagne.

During the entire meal he kept up a running conversation. Everything from politics to art and most things in between. I didn't say much and neither did Simone.

It was only when I stood up to leave that he suddenly said, "You read the file? You've seen Zingari? What do you think?"

I said, "It's possible. It could be done with the right organization and workforce."

There was genuine astonishment on his face. "You mean you've found a way in?"

"There's always a way in if you think hard enough." I helped myself to more champagne. "Even the Bank of England. In fact a long time ago someone did just that."

He nodded slowly. "All right, how?"

"That comes later. First I have to see a man called Aldo Barzini."

"Why?"

"Because for this kind of job he's the best there is."

He reached for a cigar and the waiter lit it for him. "And what does he do when he isn't working, this Barzini?"

"Runs a funeral business in Palermo among other things."

He laughed helplessly, his whole body shaking. "By God, but you're a rogue, sir. I knew it the minute I clapped eyes on you." He wiped his face with a napkin. "All right, go to Palermo and see this man. Justin can fly you up there in the Cessna in the morning."

"I want Barzini and probably two others. I'm hoping he'll be able to provide specialists. That kind of thing comes expensive."

"How much?"

"That depends how rich he is these days." I shrugged. "Sixty, maybe seventy-five thousand dollars for the team. This is a knife-edge proposition, remember. One step and we all go down."

"I will honor any agreement you make," he said calmly. "Justin will have my personal draft for twenty-five thousand dollars in his pocket as a down payment. Will that satisfy this Barzini?"

"I should think so." I stood up. "I don't want Langley getting into my hair. Is that understood?"

"Perfectly." He raised his glass and smiled beautifully. "Goodnight to you, Major Grant."

I left them to it and moved back through the garden toward my own room. It started to rain, a fine spray blowing in on the wind, but enough to freshen the heavy atmosphere and to perfume the night with the scent of flowers.

I lay on the divan by the open french windows gazing out into the night and smoked a cigarette. After a while, I must have dozed because I came awake suddenly and was instantly aware of two things. That it was raining very heavily indeed and that my sister was playing the piano somewhere not too far away.

It was a Bach Prelude, scintillating, ice-cold stuff, perfectly played and perfectly in keeping with the circumstances. 1 found an old raincoat in the wardrobe, draped it over my shoulders and went out on the terrace.

Sheet lightning flickered far out to sea, thunder rumbled menacingly overhead and the rain increased into a solid drenching downpour as I moved through the garden, following the sound of the piano.

I mounted to the high terrace and approached the library where I had first seen her, but she was not there. I moved on, climbing steps to another terrace, conscious of the murmur of voices.

Shutters stood partially open to the night, a white gauze curtain billowed in the wind. When I peered inside, Dimitri Stavrou was seated on the edge of a large four-poster bed. Simone was standing in front of him and his hands were busy. I could see her face reflected in the mirror on the far wall and she looked about as wretched as any human being could. In other circumstances I might have felt sorry for her, but Hannah was my only consideration now.

I moved on through the rain, following the sound of music and mounted some marble steps to another broad terrace protected by a striped canvas sun awning from which rain dropped steadily. French windows stood open to the night, and inside Hannah sat at a grand piano.

I approached cautiously. There seemed to be no one else around and I was filled with a sudden wild hope that I might grab her and be out of there before Stavrou and his friends realized what had hit them.

And then thunder rumbled menacingly in the distance again, only it was deep down in the dog's throat this time, and the Doberman stood up beside the piano stool, stiff-legged, and eyed me coldly.

Hannah turned to stare out into the rain toward me. "Is anyone there?" she called.

Frau Kubel stepped into view and saw me at once. A hand disappeared inside her white apron and reappeared clutching an automatic with a six-inch silencer on the end. To my horror, she pointed it at the back of Hannah's skull and stared fixedly toward me, not saying a word, the same grim expression on her face.

My blood ran cold and I hastily raised both hands, palms toward her. She lowered the automatic, but still held it against her thigh, gazing toward me.

A hand tugged at my sleeve, I turned and found Langley at my elbow. "Very naughty, old stick," he whispered cheerfully. "I mean, there could have been a very nasty accident there."

"You go to hell," I said and I brushed past him and moved back through the garden to my room.

I stripped off my wet clothes and lay on the bed thinking about things, thoroughly angry with myself for being so stupid. I didn't hear her enter, but when lightning flickered out to sea, it pulled Simone out of the darkness by the window. I didn't say a word; simply stood up and walked toward her. Her dress was soaked and clung to her body like a second skin. I started to unbutton it.

"What were his orders?" I said. "Anything I wanted? Anything to keep me happy?"

"Damn you to hell!" She struck me across the face, struggling in my grasp. "Justin came and told him what happened a little while ago. She could have been killed. Your sister could have been killed. He means it, you fool. Every word of it. Don't you understand that?"

My fingers were busy with the last few buttons. I peeled the wet dress away gently and dropped it to the floor. She started to cry violently, collapsing into my arms.

"It's all right," I said, gentling her. "Everything's going to be all right."

She came to bed with me then with no further fuss and cried for a long time as she lay there in the dark in my arms, although whether for me or for herself, or for both of us, was not made plain.

Finally she fell asleep, her head on my chest, and I lay there holding her, watching the lightning flicker on the horizon, trying to decide in my own mind just exactly how I intended to kill Dimitri Stavrou when the time came.

CHAPTER FOUR

RAIN ON THE DEAD

THE CESSNA WAS MOORED TO A couple of buoys in the horseshoe bay at the foot of the cliffs beneath the villa. It was reached by a winding dirt road and Moro took me down there in a Landrover just before nine.

It was a poor sort of day, heavy gray clouds dropping in over the cliffs, mist rolling off the sea, pushing rain before it. Bonetti waited at the wheel of a speedboat moored beside the stone jetty, the engine already ticking over and Justin Langley stood on the edge, smoking a cigarette and looking out to sea. He turned as I approached, a slightly theatrical figure in his fur-lined boots and old flying jacket.

As I got out of the Landrover I said, "I just bet you've got a shoulder holster inside that thing, too. What are we playing this morning? Dawn Patrol?"

He smiled good-humoredly. "Now don't be like that, old stick. After all, you are in my hands, so to speak."

"Well, don't forget I'm precious cargo." I looked out at the mist rolling in through the entrance. "What about the weather?"

"The weather?" He squinted up into the rain. "Well, that's something that's always with us, isn't it? Like death. Now if you would kindly get into the boat, maybe we could get started. I've a little business myself in Palermo I'd like to fit in if there's time."

"I just bet you have," I said. "What is he—blond or brunette?"

That languid smile of his was wiped clean and for a moment there was murder in the eyes. Stupid of me under the circumstances, but it was done now. I brushed past him and went down the steps to the speedboat. He followed me, cast off, and Bonetti took us out to the Cessna.

When we reached her, I scrambled out first onto the nearest float, climbed into the cabin and buckled myself into the passenger seat. There was a moment's delay before Langley followed me. The speedboat sheered off and he went through the usual routine check and started the engine. Everything sounded fine.

He turned and smiled. "All right, old stick?"

"I don't see why not," I said, although I suppose I should have known better.

"Good," he said and started to taxi downwind slowly, leaning out of the window, peering into the mist.

And then quite suddenly, he gave it everything it had, and we were away, lifting far too soon. The nose dropped, but he'd enough sense not to pull back on the stick until he had the power.

We roared across the harbor no more than twenty feet above the water straight into that wall of mist and then the engine note deepened and he started to climb at just the right moment.

We came up out of the mist through dirty white cloud, rain rattling against the windscreen. He took a cigarette from behind his ear and stuck it in his mouth.

"Beautiful," I said, clenching my hands to stop their trembling. "Nice and fast and showy. And one of these days you're going to kill yourself doing it."

He laughed out loud. "Well, you must admit it's fun trying."

We came up through the clouds into clear air, he stamped on the right rudder and swung slowly north, turning inland.

As for me, I turned up the collar of my trenchcoat, another item thoughtfully provided as part of my general wardrobe, closed my eyes and pretended to sleep and after a while, did just that.

Not too far out of Palermo on the coast road to Messina you come to the beaches of Romagnolo, a favorite weekend spot for city dwellers, only not today. It had been dirty weather all the way, heavy rain had cleared the beaches and there was a whole lot more of that nasty, gray mist rolling in off the water.

It didn't seem to bother Langley in the slightest. He simply sat there at the controls whistling softly between his teeth until a few miles along the coast from Romagnolo he said suddenly, "Going down, and I'd hang on if I were you. Could be a trifle bumpy."

It must have qualified for the understatement of the year. We skimmed the shoulder of a mountain, narrowly avoiding some sort of baroque palace and plunged into a wide bay beyond as the first gray strands curled along the tips of the wings. A final burst of power to level out in the descent and we dropped into calm water with a splash.

Mist closed in around us and Langley said cheerfully, "All right, old stick?"

"One of life's great experiences," I assured him.

I opened the window beside me and peered out as we taxied forward. The tip of a floating pontoon suddenly pushed out of the mist; Langley cut the engine and we drifted in. As I got the door open and stepped across with the line Langley handed me, a man in a black oilskin and stocking cap appeared from the mist. He had a dark saturnine face and badly needed a shave. Rather incongruously he was carrying an umbrella which he handed to me, relieving me in turn of the line.

I stood holding the umbrella in the pouring rain, wondering what in the hell was keeping Langley and then he scrambled out of the cabin and I saw that he had changed out of his flying kit and was now wearing suede boots and a navy blue nylon raincoat.

"Right, off we go, old stick," he said, completely ignoring the man in the black oilskin and we started along the swaying pontoon through the torrential rain, both sheltering under the umbrella. The baroque palace I had glimpsed from the air loomed out of the mist up there on the side of the mountain.

"Another of Stavrou's weekend places?" I asked.

"Don't be bitter, old stick," Langley said. "It just isn't you."

We crossed a shingle beach to a black Mercedes limousine parked at the end of a narrow asphalt road. As we approached, a uniformed chauffeur emerged and opened the rear door. He took the umbrella as we got in.

He slid behind the wheel and waited. Langley pulled down a flap at the bottom of the dividing screen, took out a bottle and a couple of glasses into each of which he poured a generous measure of an excellent brandy.

He toasted me. "You took that rather well, old stick. You know for an American, you're not half bad. Very strange." He poured himself another one. "On the other hand, you did go to Winchester, didn't you? I suppose that explains it."

To which there could really be no answer and before I could even try, he said casually, "Where to?"

"I thought you were supposed to keep out of my hair?"

"But I will, old stick. Honestly." He even managed to look hurt as he took a foolscap envelope from his inside pocket. "On the other hand, considering what's inside this I should have thought your friend Barzini would be enchanted to make my acquaintance."

I decided to play along with him for the time being, mainly because I'd been expecting something like this anyway. I said, "All right, Via San Marco. It's off the Via Roma near the central railway station and tell him to go through the Piazza Pretoria."

He gave the order over the intercom in Italian and as the Mercedes moved away I, too, helped myself to more brandy. We drove up from the beach, passing the palace or whatever the hell it was supposed to be, at some distance and turned out through some large ironwork gates onto the main Messina-Palermo coast road.

Langley lit a cigarette. "This Barzini, what's so good about him?"

"For a start he's sixty-three years of age," I said. "An advantage when I consider the younger generation."

He refused to be thrown. "In other words, he's a survivor."

I hesitated for a moment and then continued. "That file you had on me, it mentioned a job I did in Albania a few years ago."

"When you pulled the U2 pilot out of the prison in Tirana?"

"There was a little more to it than that. Aldo Barzini was an underwater saboteur with the Italian Navy during the war."

Langley looked interested. "Human torpedoes and so on?"

I nodded. "He sank two British destroyers in Port Said back in 1942. When I met him, he was smuggling cigarettes, penicillin, stuff like that, making regular runs from Brindisi to Albania. He was hired to give me and my team a way out. In the original plan he was supposed to wait two nights in a cove on the Albanian coast about thirty miles from Tirana. Then he got a coded message on his radio telling him we'd been sold out. Ordering him to make a run for it."

"And did he?"

"No, he landed, stole a car and made straight for a farm about fifteen miles inland that he knew we were using as a rendezvous. Arrived about ten minutes in front of the *Sigurmi*. That's the Albanian secret police. They could have given the Gestapo pointers, believe me."

"So you got out?"

"Only just and only because of Barzini."

"Quite a man," Langley said. "What does he do now, besides bury people?"

"Plays the best guitar I've heard in my life. Sells guns to the Israelis, guns to the Arabs. For all I know he's even running them in for the IRA. A citizen of the world, or so he keeps telling me. No favorites. The one thing he won't touch is drugs. He had a nephew on heroin who died rather unpleasantly."

"A sentimentalist into the bargain. Now there's an interesting combination."

"You could say that. As a matter of record, the man who ran the drug scene in the town where the boy lived was found on a hook in the local slaughter house. Somebody'd cut his throat."

"My God, but that's beautiful." For once, there was sincere admiration in Langley's voice.

We turned into the Piazza Pretoria and I rapped on the partition quickly. As the Mercedes braked to a halt, I got out and walked across to the incredible baroque fountains, surrounded by water nymphs, tritons, and the lesser gods.

Langley joined me, holding the umbrella against the pouring rain. "What's the attraction?"

"This," I said. "I've always had a weakness for it. It's so incredibly vulgar. Just like life—a bad joke. I'm going to walk the rest of the way. It isn't far."

I crossed the square without a backward glance. I suppose he must have turned back to tell the driver to follow because I'd almost reached the other side before he caught up with me.

The rain was torrential now, bouncing from the cobbles and he held the umbrella over both of us. "And what in the hell are we supposed to be doing now?" he asked amiably.

"Walking in the rain," I told him. "I've always liked walking in the rain, ever since I was a kid."

"And keeping out the world," he said. "I know the feeling."

I was surprised, perhaps it would be more accurate to say, disturbed to find that we might actually have something in common. I tried not to show it.

"But life isn't like that, is it?" I shrugged. "Like I said, just a bad joke."

I felt unaccountably depressed and I think the feeling must have touched him also. Certainly he didn't attempt to make any further conversation. We passed the beautiful old church of Santa Caterina, turned into the Via Roma and walked toward the central station.

The Via San Marco was a narrow cobbled street, old eighteenth-century houses five or six stories high towering up on either side. It was a quiet place, somehow cut off from the noise of city traffic. About halfway along, an old-fashioned horse-drawn hearse waited at the curb, draped in black crepe, black plumes on the horses' heads wilting in the rain. The driver wore a caped greatcoat and a top hat, banded with more black crepe, the tails hanging down over his neck. It was the kind of thing you still saw in Sicily and probably nowhere else on earth.

Four men in green baize aprons manhandled an ornate coffin with gilt handles out of a doorway and into the hearse. One of them closed the glass door and crossed himself. The driver flicked his whip and the horses moved away, plumes nodding.

The sign over the door was discreet and simple. *Aldo Barzini — Undertaker.* Gold leaf on a black background. The Mercedes pulled into the curb and we got out and passed inside.

The hall was panelled in mahogany and lit by candles. There was an image of the Virgin in an alcove on the right, grave, unsmiling, and the air was heavy with the scent of flowers and incense. Strangely unpleasant, that smell, as if it were trying to hide something.

I rang a small brass handbell that stood on a table. It echoed faintly and almost immediately, a tiny, desiccated man in an old-fashioned dark suit and winged collar, appeared noiselessly from a door to the right.

He adjusted his spectacles and blinked nervously. "Signors! How may I be of service?"

I said in my best Italian, "I'm looking for Signor Barzini. A personal matter. We're old friends."

He shrugged helplessly. "What can I say, signor, you've just missed him. Each week at this time he takes flowers to his nephew's grave at the Capuchin cemetery on Monte Pellegrino."

"How long will he be?"

"Who knows, signor. An hour, maybe two. Perhaps you gentlemen would care to wait."

"For God's sake, not that, old stick," Langley said hurriedly. "I don't think I could stand the smell."

I expressed my thanks to the old man, told him we'd be back, and we got out quickly.

The cemetery was deserted in the rain, but a yellow Alfa Romeo was parked in the outer courtyard, a uniformed chauffeur at the wheel. He had the face of a good middleweight fighter and he glanced up casually as Langley and I got out of the Mercedes, then returned to his magazine.

"Is he Barzini's man?" Langley asked me as we moved through the entrance into the cloisters.

"I don't know. I've never seen him before."

An Arab fountain lifted into the air, trying to beat the rain at its own game and failed. We moved on through another archway and found ourselves in the cemetery itself. It was not very large and was ringed by cypress trees, the whole area crowded with fantastic monuments, ornate gothic shrines, and family vaults in marble and bronze.

We found him with no trouble, standing in front of a black marble tomb with bronze eternity doors. He was wearing a white Burberry trenchcoat and rain hat, which didn't surprise me. Buying all his clothes in England was one of his affectations.

I said to Langley, "You stay here," and started forward and in the same moment the chauffeur, whom I'd last seen sitting behind the wheel of the Alfa, stepped from behind a tomb on my right holding a Sterling sub-machine gun in both hands.

Barzini swung round and I raised my hands and called in English, "It's me, Aldo. Oliver Grant."

He smiled instantly. "Oliver, baby, what's new?"

He spoke English with a strong American accent, relic of a boyhood spent in New York where his parents had emigrated for a time and laced with strange, anachronistic slang like something out of a pulp magazine of the thirties.

He said to the chauffeur, "It's all right, Luigi. Back to the car."

The chauffeur moved away and when he was close enough, Barzini gave me the full embrace including a smacking kiss on each cheek to show I was considered family.

He held me away from him and I could feel the strength in those hands. "You're looking good, boy. Where've you been keeping yourself?"

"Here and there," I said. "You don't look any older. You must keep a portrait in the attic or something." He frowned in puzzlement and I added hastily, "An English joke."

He thumped his chest and grinned. "I'm fine. Never been better. Different girl every night."

He roared with laughter and took out a cheap Egyptian cheroot. It was really quite amazing. He just didn't seem to age. Although there was a silver hair or two in the sweeping moustache, the face was tanned and healthy and the teeth were as bad as ever. Some things never changed.

He glanced over my shoulder at Langley. "Who's your friend?"

"No friend, Aldo," I said. "I'm in trouble. Bad trouble."

His face went very still and the gray eyes suddenly had the same sort of shine that you get when light gleams on the edge of a cut throat razor. "And you came to me, boy? That's good. I like that. Tell me about it."

He gave me one of those vile Egyptian cheroots of his and we sat on the edge of a tomb and I told him the whole story. As I talked, he kept eyeing Langley who waited at the end of the path twenty or thirty yards away, sheltering under the umbrella.

When I was finished he said softly, "And this is one of them, this bastard here?"

I nodded.

He said, "I know of this Stavrou. A big man with Mafia in the States, but not anymore. Why don't you let me get a few friends together and we'll all go down to Capo Passero and break his skull."

"It wouldn't work," I said. "My sister's on borrowed time now. I've got to go through with it. It's the only way."

"It's possible, then?"

"I think so."

"Good." He smiled cheerfully. "We'll go back to my place and you tell me how we're going to do it."

I don't think I've ever felt so relieved in my life as I turned and followed him along the path. As we reached Langley he grinned, "Everything all right, old stick?"

Barzini looked him over. "And this is one of them, this girl-boy?" He shook his head. "Mother of God, what's the world coming to?" He took me by the arm, dismissing Langley completely and said as we moved away, "You know, my friend, there are days when I feel like climbing into one of my own coffins and pulling down the lid."

CHAPTER FIVE

A Special Kind
of Woman

I DROVE BACK TO PALERMO IN the Alfa with Barzini, and when we reached the funeral premises in Via San Marco we found that Langley had beaten us to it and was standing waiting on the pavement beside the Mercedes.

"Ah, there you are, old stick," he said as I got out. "What kept you?"

Barzini remained unimpressed. "I don't like him," he said. "His smile—it's like a brass plate on a coffin. You're sure you want this pig along?"

For once Langley looked as if he didn't know what in the hell to say next. I said, "He's the banker, remember."

"All right," Barzini said grudgingly and prodded Langley in the chest with a stubby forefinger. "Only mind your manners and keep your mouth shut."

We followed him along the candlelit hall; he opened the door at the rear and we passed through into some sort of preparation room. There were corpses laid out, some of them being worked on by morticians. Most of them wore new clothes and the faces had been carefully made up to create some semblance of life.

Barzini paused briefly to make a suggestion to an old man who was working on the face of a little girl of perhaps seven or eight, then continued on his way calmly. Langley didn't look too happy and I wasn't exactly delighted with the whole thing myself.

But things were going downhill fast, for when Barzini opened another door, we followed him through into an immense arched room dimly lit, heavy with the scent of flowers. There were rows of coffins on either side, each with an occupant.

At the far end of the room wooden steps lifted to a small glass office. Barzini mounted them briskly and a uniformed man sitting at a desk inside stood to greet him.

"These gentlemen and I have business to discuss, Guido," he said. "Go and have something to eat. Take an hour."

Guido saluted and made himself scarce and Barzini closed the door after him. Langley gazed down through the glass window in fascinated horror at the rows of corpses below.

"You like it?" Barzini said. "You want I should find a place for you? We call it the Waiting Hall. You'd be surprised how many people have a pathological fear of being buried alive. They like to be certain, so we leave them here for a while. Notice the cord running into each coffin. One end connected to a bell, the other to a ring on the corpse's finger. The slightest movement and a bell sounds up here. That's why we have an attendant day and night."

There was a moment's silence when he finished and then, quite distinctly, one of the bells above his head tinkled.

"Good God Almighty!" Langley exclaimed, genuine horror on his face, and his hand dipped inside his coat and came out holding a Walther PPK.

Barzini laughed harshly. "And just what do you think you're going to do with that?" he demanded and pushed it aside with the back of his hand.

He opened the door and went down the steps quickly. We watched him cross to a coffin and examine a corpse. The bell tinkled faintly again, he turned and came back.

"Nothing to worry about. Those warning bells are so sensitive that the least movement of the corpse sets them going."

Langley's forehead was beaded with sweat and his eyes were wild. "Does it ever happen for real?" he whispered.

"Twice last year. A middle-aged woman sat up in her shroud in the middle of the night and started screaming." Langley's eyes almost started from his head and Barzini patted his cheek and grinned delightedly. "See, Oliver, he isn't so tough after all."

He sat on the edge of the desk and pushed another of those lousy Egyptian cheroots into his mouth. "Let's have it. How do we do this job?"

"All right," I said. "Getting there is no problem. We can go in by boat with the kind of front that would be acceptable to anybody."

"And the prison?"

"Something else again."

I described it in detail and when I'd finished, he frowned. "It sounds like Fort Knox to me. And you say you've got a way in?"

"I think so. The cliffs on the seaward side are about one hundred and fifty feet high. Supposedly impregnable. Because of that they never have more than two guards on the ramparts."

"Are you trying to say you think they could be climbed?"

"If someone on the ramparts was in place to throw down a line at the right moment and pull up a climbing rope. And I'll need a number two. Preferably the sort of guy who's at home on a rock face."

"But you've still got to get somebody inside to be on the ramparts at the right time," Langley said. "I mean, it's just not on. They don't even let civilians into the bloody place to work."

"Oh, yes, they do," I turned to Barzini. "Every Friday night a local operator named Zingari, who's now working for us, sends in a couple of truckloads of women to amuse the troops, special dispensation of Colonel Masmoudi who always has first choice and never fails to pick less than two according to Zingari."

Barzini seemed amused. "And you're suggesting that your inside operator should be a woman? Someone who would gain access by passing herself off as a whore?"

"No great trick in that. Zingari, as I said, is working for us and he told me himself he's always having to bring fresh girls in from Tripoli."

Langley laughed wildly. "For God's sake, Grant, you're living in cloud cuckoo land. Do you realize what you're asking for? A woman able to pass as a whore, willing to act as one if the going gets rough, capable of disposing of two armed sentries on the north wall."

I said, "It would take an exceptional woman, I grant you, but it's the only way, believe me. The one flaw in their security. The only one."

Barzini laughed harshly. "I like it and it's just crazy enough to work, but as you say, one would need an exceptional woman."

"And I suppose you just happen to have one in mind?" Langley said sourly.

Barzini sighed heavily. "No faith, that's the trouble with you young people today." He turned to me. "There's a girl called Angel Carter appearing at the Tabu this week. That's a beach club on the way to Romagnolo. A new business interest of mine. First show seven-thirty. I'll introduce you tonight. You'll find her rather unusual."

"Fine," I said. "I'll buy that, but what about my other requirement?"

"Someone who's good on a cliff face?" he said. "A climber who's also willing to cut throats? An unusual combination." He hesitated. "Did I ever tell you about my nephew, Nino, my brother's boy?"

"I don't think so."

"The original wild one. They sent him to university, but he got thrown out. Did his military service in the Alps with a mountain regiment, then came home and killed a man in a quarrel over some stupid girl."

"What happened?"

"He took to the *maquis*. Lived as a bandit in the Cammarata mountains for almost three years. I finally got him a pardon for his mother's sake by laying out a little money."

"Where is he now?"

"That's the trouble, he's on the run again. The Mafia this time." Barzini sighed and shook his head. "Would you believe it, but he has to choose the daughter of the Capo Mafia of all Sicily to put in the family way. Ten thousand dollars for anyone who brings in his head. Believe me there haven't been so many looking for one man since the days of Guiliano."

"From the sound of things I'd say he'd be glad of a way out. How do we get hold of him?"

"A phone call to the right person is all it takes."

As he lifted the receiver, the bell tinkled and Langley started violently. Barzini laughed. "Why don't you go and make the check this time, Mr. Langley?"

Langley glared helplessly at him and Barzini was still laughing as he dialed the number.

In Sicily on All Saints' Day the children are given presents from the dead and the graves are probably the best kept in the world. In a society so concerned with death it is not surprising to discover that there are at least eight thousand corpses in the catacombs. But the state of affairs at the Capuchin Zita Church was even more interesting. It was a place much visited by tourists and Barzini's informant had insisted on meeting him there face-to-face, just to make sure he was talking to the right person before disclosing Nino's whereabouts.

There was no sign of anyone when we got there, only a verger in soiled black cassock who swept the floor.

"I'll wait here," Barzini said. "You two might as well have a look below while you're here. You'll find it very interesting."

We went down some steps into a high room—an enormously high room. I think it was one of the most horrible sights I have ever seen in my life. The shelves were piled high with desiccated corpses, all with name plates around their necks. Some were skeletons, some had flesh on their bones, eyes that stared, tufted hair.

We left in a hurry and I think Langley was fractionally ahead as we went up the stairs. Barzini was standing in the centre of the church making a note in a pocket diary.

"You lousy bastard," Langley said.

"Didn't you like it?" Barzini shrugged. "The aristocracy of Palermo. Do you know that people come on Sundays to point out their ancestors?"

"To hell with their bloody ancestors," Langley said. "What's happened to this guy you were supposed to see?"

"You mean the verger?" Barzini said. "I've already spoken to him. He's just gone. Nino will be waiting at a *trattoria* on the other side of the village of Misilmeri on the road to Agrigento. Better to make it after dark so I said ten o'clock. That gives us nice time to see Angel Carter."

He turned and walked out and we followed, utterly defeated.

You could hear Club Tabu from a long way away and the car park was almost full in spite of the fact that it was so early in the evening.

Once inside, you could have been in London, Paris or Las Vegas. The decor and design of such places is the same the world over along with the steaks straight from the freezer and the packaged food. There was a casino which seemed to be doing good business and up on the stage a trio played modern jazz brilliantly although nobody seemed to be paying much attention.

We settled ourselves at the bar and had a drink. Barzini glanced at his watch. "Not long now, then you'll see what I mean."

A few moments later there was a drum roll and a compere came on stage to announce the commencement of the floor show. The effect was remarkable. The casino emptied of all but the most hardened gamblers and there was a general rush for seats.

A larger orchestra now took their places on the stand and someone checked the mike. A moment later the compere ran on to a drum roll and announced in four languages that the Club Tabu was proud and happy to present, straight from her sensational run at the Moulin Rouge in Paris, Miss Angel Carter.

He ran for the wings, the lights went out completely. A single spot picked her out of the darkness, one of the most beautiful girls I'd ever clapped eyes on, long blonde hair hanging straight to the shoulders, a simple green silk mini dress with pleated skirt, black stockings, gold shoes with enormously high heels.

When she started to sing, you'd have thought it was Judy Garland come down to earth again. The same emotion deep in the throat, the same way of breaking a note in two so that it sent something crawling up your spine.

She started to work her way through all the old standards. *A Foggy Day, September Song, The Lady is a Tramp,* and had them eating out of her hand, especially the men when she moved out along the boardwalk above the heads of the audience.

I said to Barzini, "Listen, she's fantastic, but what in the hell am I supposed to do with her except the obvious thing? She wouldn't last five minutes on the kind of caper we're contemplating."

"Oh, I wouldn't be too sure about that," he said. "She has certain unusual qualities. Anyway, I'd like you to meet her, so we'd better get round to the back now. She only has one more number to do."

We pushed our way through the crowd to one side and negotiated the stage door with no difficulty as Barzini was obviously known. Angel Carter's name was on the door of a dressing room in a corridor at the rear and we walked outside. She was still singing up there on the stage, presumably an encore. When she finished, the audience stamped and cheered again, but this time it didn't do them any good. The band broke into a fast quickstep and a moment later she came down the steps.

As she reached the bottom, an astonishing thing happened. Two men in evening dress who had been standing there talking in low tones suddenly grabbed her.

The larger one, a thoroughly nasty-looking specimen, said in Italian, "Okay, baby, you're coming out with us tonight."

"Definitely!" the other one said and ran a hand up her skirt.

They were both obviously pretty drunk. I took a step forward and Barzini pulled me back. Angel Carter pulled free and delivered a high karate kick to the big man's jaw and the effect of that stiletto heel was devastating. At the same time, she put a knee into the other man's gut and gave it him again in the face as he keeled over.

Such was the vigor of the movement that her blond wig came off and all was revealed, for underneath was a very old-fashioned GI haircut. Angel Carter was a man.

He stamped down the corridor, clutching the blond wig and cursing fluently in very explicit Anglo-Saxon.

"Good evening, Angelo," Barzini said.

Carter stopped dead and glared at him, "And what in the hell's good about it? I'm sick of getting touched up by drunken bums every night. I quit. If you've got anything better to offer, come in. If you haven't, get lost."

He walked into the dressing room, skirt swirling, and slammed the door.

Barzini grinned. "Like I said, a very exceptional woman." He opened the door and we followed him in.

Angelo Carter was seated at a dressing table dialing a phone number. A cigarette dangled from the corner of his mouth. Barzini gave him a light and Carter started to speak in rapid and fluent Italian to some girl called Rosanna, telling her that he'd be calling just after midnight.

"His mother was Italian, which explains the Angelo," Barzini said. "Father, American."

Angelo slammed down the receiver, reached for a bottle of Scotch and poured about three fingers into a tumbler. Barzini said, "So you're going to do the second show?"

"Only because I owe you," Angelo said. "But, after that, finish. Final and definite." He swallowed half his whisky and looked across at Langley and me. "What's this supposed to be? Open night?"

"I'd like you to meet a good friend of mine, Major Grant," Barzini said. "You've got a lot in common."

"No, I haven't," Angelo said firmly. "Not with any major I ever heard of."

"You were both in Vietnam."

Angelo was about to finish the rest of his whisky. Instead he paused and eyed me speculatively. "You were in Nam? What outfit?"

"Special Services Executive," I told him.

"Jesus!" He turned to Barzini. "That's the military branch of the Mafia. You're in bad company, Aldo."

"Angelo was in the Green Berets," Barzini said. "I always understood they cut a neat throat, isn't that so, Oliver?"

"So they say." I lit a cigarette and said to Angelo, "A long way from the Mekon."

"Don't rub it in, friend," he said. "I did a drag act in a troop show when I was in a Saigon military hospital, just for laughs. It was supposed to be a one-night stand and here I am, three years later, the toast of Europe." He shook his head.

"No, Aldo, I'll do your second show for you, but after that, you'll never see me in skirts again."

He tossed back the rest of his whisky and Barzini picked up the bottle and poured him another. "That's a pity, Angelo, because I've got a new contract for you and the terms are really quite excellent."

"They always are," Angelo told him sourly.

"Twenty thousand dollars," Barzini said. "Only one performance required."

Angelo grinned. "You've got to be joking. What do I have to do? Kill somebody?"

"Very probably."

There was a longish silence. Angelo stopped smiling, glanced at Langley and me and back to Barzini. "This is for real?"

"Of course."

Angelo said rapidly in Italian, "Who are these guys? What goes on?"

"A waste of time," Barzini replied. "They both speak Italian."

"Look, we're not asking you to rob a bank," I put in. "Just help get someone out of a Libyan prison."

Angelo jumped up and made a cutting gesture with one hand. He nodded towards Barzini. "Him I trust, you two I don't know. Outside."

I responded to Barzini's slight nod by opening the door and leading the way out. Langley was annoyed and showed it. "If I had my way ..."

"Which you don't," I said. "So your opinion's of no interest."

He walked away angrily and I leaned against the wall beside the door and waited, listening to the murmur of voices inside. I don't think it even occurred to me that Angelo would say no, and not just because of my faith in Barzini's powers of persuasion. The boy was ripe for change, it was as simple as that. Like me, he'd been in the Hole for too long. It was unlikely that he'd turn down any kind of a chance to break out.

The door opened suddenly and Barzini said, "Come in."

Angelo was standing by the dressing table and he was still not wearing the wig. There was a moment's silence and then he raised his glass. "I must be crazy, but here's to crime."

An enormous feeling of relief surged through me, but before I could say anything Barzini glanced at his watch. "We'll have to be moving if we're to get to the other side of Misilmeri on time." He turned to Angelo, "Meet us at my place in the Via San Marco when you've done your second show."

"Nothing doing," Angelo told him. "I've got a date with a very willing lady."

"She'll have to wait."

"But can I, that's the point?"

Langley said, "I suppose it all depends what you're trying to prove."

Angelo looked him over and the eyes beneath the fringed lashes were cold. "I don't have to prove a thing, friend. What's your story?" Langley took a step toward him and Barzini grabbed him by the arm, opened the door and shoved him outside. "Around midnight then," he said to Angelo. "We'll expect you."

He closed the door and I turned to Langley, who was standing against the wall, hands thrust deep into his pockets, feet apart. I said, "You're along for the ride, that's all, so keep your mouth shut. Open it again like that and I'll close it for you personally."

And once again he did the unexpected thing by smiling sweetly. "Why, thanks, old stick, I'll try and remember that. I really will."

He turned and walked out and we followed.

We left the yellow Alfa Romeo parked conspicuously outside the funeral premises on the Via San Marco and left by the rear entrance. Barzini led us briskly through a maze of narrow streets and we finally emerged at the back of the central station where Langley's chauffeur was waiting in the Mercedes. We got in quickly and he drove away.

"Do you think that's enough?" I said.

"That yellow Alfa of mine is one of the best known cars in Palermo. Someone could be watching. They all know my relationship to Nino. Not that the Mafia would try anything with me personally, you understand. They know better. But they want the boy." He shrugged, apparently quite unconcerned. "We'll have to see."

It was still raining and there wasn't much traffic on the Agrigento road. Just the occasional group of peasants coming into Palermo early to secure a good pitch for tomorrow's market. Old women in long skirts and shawls, baskets on their heads, strange, medieval figures, walking behind heavily laden donkeys. Nothing changed, it seemed, and I felt unaccountably depressed.

The streets of Misilmeri were clear, but the wineshop seemed to be doing a good enough trade, people sitting inside out of the rain. There had been lights behind us for some time and Barzini leaned forward and told the driver to slow. A cattle truck pulled out to pass us and moved on into the night.

"Good!" He relaxed and sat back again. "We're almost there. Are you armed?"

I shook my head. "No."

"Try this for size." He handed me a Smith and Wesson .38 Special and turned to Langley.

"Everything in perfect working order, old stick," Langley said. "Are we expecting trouble?"

"I always do," Barzini told him. "That's why I'm still around."

He leaned over to give the driver further instructions and a moment later we turned into a dirt road and started to climb through a forest of pine trees.

The *trattoria* was at the top of the hill in the trees, a typical back-country inn, a poor sort of place surrounded by crumbling walls. We drove in through an archway. From the looks of things there had once been a formal garden here, but it had obviously been allowed to run wild over the years and crowded in on the house.

We stopped in a small courtyard at the bottom of steps leading up to a terrace. The door stood wide open, light flooding out. Someone was playing the guitar and I don't mean striking the odd chord or two. The fingerwork was really quite exceptional.

Langley said in genuine astonishment, "My God, isn't that Bach?"

"The Fugue in G minor," Barzini said. "Originally composed for the lute and transcribed for the guitar into A minor. A favorite of the great Segovia." He listened for a moment and nodded. "He's improving."

The playing stopped as we went up the steps, Barzini leading the way into a large, square room with a beamed ceiling. There were two or three rough wooden tables with benches and a zinc-topped bar with a guitar on it.

The innkeeper, a bent old man in a soiled white apron was serving wine to a couple of men sitting in the far corner, rough looking specimens, typical of the younger men still to be found in the back country. Features brutalized and coarsened by a life of toil, shabby patched clothing, broken boots, cloth caps. They wore bandoliers around their waists. One of them had a shot gun across his knees, the other had his on the bench close to hand. They could have been gamekeepers off one of the big country estates, but I didn't think it likely.

Langley took up position by the door, a hand in his pocket. I followed Barzini to the bar and leaned against it casually, facing them. They stared at us woodenly and for a moment there was only the silence and then the old man shuffled forward and dusted a table with a dirty cloth.

"Your pleasure, signores?"

Barzini picked up the guitar, tuned the E string slightly and started to play the Bach Fugue. It was really quite incredible. If what we had just heard was good, then this was brilliant by any standards. Even the two hard boys in the corner sat up and took notice.

Barzini stopped playing and called, "How many times do I have to tell you, Nino? The fourth finger, not the third on that run. With you, it's like putting your foot on the brake each time."

He moved in through the door at the side of the bar, a slight, wiry young man in a patched corduroy suit and leather leggings, a carbine over his shoulder, finger on the trigger. The face beneath the cloth cap was recklessly handsome in spite of the week-old stubble of beard.

"Heh, Uncle Aldo," he said. "What kept you?"

Barzini opened his arms, Nino put the rifle down on top of the bar and they embraced.

"God, but you stink like a pig, boy." Barzini shoved him away. "Thank God your dear mother isn't alive to see you now."

"What do you expect?" Nino shrugged. "I've been living like one for weeks."

The innkeeper brought a bottle of wine and glasses. Barzini said as he filled them, "That's all over now. I've come to take you out. I need you."

Nino paused, glass in hand. "You mean you've patched things up with them?"

"Unfortunately no, but I've got work for you."

"Not the business? Not that?" Nino groaned. "You know I can't stand all those corpses."

Barzini turned to me in disgust. "You see what I mean about the youth of today? He doesn't mind killing them just so long as he doesn't have to look at the bodies afterward." He cuffed Nino, knocking his cap off. "Ingrate. This is my friend, Major Grant. You're going to help us get someone out of prison." He patted his cheek. "If you're a good boy there might be a little money in it for you."

Nino picked up his cap. "What do I have to do?"

"Climb a cliff face by night," I said. "A hundred and fifty feet high."

He grinned. "Now that I like. That very definitely sounds a better proposition than this." He emptied his glass and tossed it behind the bar. "Let's go then."

"Always you forget your obligations." Barzini shook his head. "These boys of yours—they've looked after you?"

"My mother couldn't have done more."

Barzini crossed to the two bravos at the corner table. Money changed hands and he came back. "Right, let's get moving."

It was still raining hard, swishing down through the trees in the garden as we moved out on to the terrace and started down the steps to the Mercedes, Barzini leading the way.

The driver got out to open the rear door and on the other side of the path, to one side, there was a trembling as if a small wind had pushed through the bushes and a rifle barrel appeared.

God knows who he was after, presumably Nino, although I didn't bother to ask. I sent Barzini sprawling with a kick in the back, drew the Smith and Wesson and fired three times, one of those instant reflex actions, the product of a good many years of hard living.

A man fell out of the bushes and lay on his face. Everyone went down and as I crouched Barzini said softly, "There'll be another."

I dodged round the back of the Mercedes and jumped into the bushes, tripping over a branch in the process and going down hard. I started to roll, every instinct telling me I'd made a bad mistake, and tried to get up.

In the same instant, a man stepped from behind a tree, a machine pistol in his hand. He wore a dark raincoat and broad-rimmed felt hat so that I couldn't see much of his face, which was a pity because I'd always wondered what Death looked like, and then the hat jumped into the air as a bullet drilled a hole between his eyes. Another shattered his jaw. He bounced from the tree and fell on his face in the long grass.

When I turned, Langley was standing at the top of the steps, perfectly balanced, feet apart, holding the Walther PPK in both hands. He lowered it slowly as I came forward.

"You might thank me, old stick," he said calmly.

"Why should I? You didn't do it for me," I said.

"Good point."

He slipped the Walther into his coat pocket as the two characters from inside the inn joined Nino and Barzini in examining the bodies.

Barzini came back to the Mercedes. "I know one of them, Cerda. He's a Mafia gun. The other's new to me. Nino's friends will put them under the sod after we've gone." He shook his head and said grimly, "God, but that was close."

"All right in the end," I said.

"Thanks to you."

"And Langley," I reminded him.

"That's right." He turned to Langley and he wasn't smiling when he said, "I can see I'm going to have to watch you after all."

"Anything else I can do to help, just call," Langley said and got into the Mercedes beside the driver.

Barzini called to Nino who joined us in the rear. We drove back down the track. As we turned on to the main road, Barzini said, "They must have been in that cattle truck that passed us outside Misilmeri. Cunning bastards." He sighed. "I'm getting old."

"Aren't we all?" I said. "Five years ago I'd have taken both of them. Tonight, I'd have died if it hadn't been for Langley."

It was a sobering thought.

It was just before midnight when we got back to Via San Marco. When we went into the entrance hall the old reception clerk appeared from his tiny room looking like some pale ghost in the guttering candlelight.

"A gentleman to see you, Signor Barzini," he said. "I put him in your office."

"Doesn't he ever go home?" I asked as we moved on.

Barzini shrugged. "Why should he? He likes it here."

He opened a mahogany door at the end of the corridor and led the way into his office. It was a beautiful room, the walls panelled in rosewood, wall-to-wall carpeting on the floor to deaden all sound. A handsome young man in a rather dashing white raincoat and tweed cap was sitting with his feet on the desk smoking what was presumably one of Barzini's best cigars.

He stood up. "What in the hell kept you? I told you, Aldo—I've got a date."

It was only when he spoke that it became apparent that this was Angelo Carter. The change was really quite incredible. He just wasn't recognizable.

"All right, all right!" Barzini said. "She can wait for another half hour, can't she?" He took off his coat and turned to me. "Okay, Oliver, you've got the floor. What do we need?"

"For a start, a good fast boat," I said. "Something that'll do twenty-five or thirty knots with no trouble like the one you used to use on the Albanian run."

"The *Palmyra*." He smiled. "Right here in Palermo harbor. No problem there. What else?"

"This man Zingari I told you about. He operates out of Zabia, which is about fifteen miles from the prison. He tells me there's a little fishing village called Gela halfway between them. Half a dozen houses, an old stone pier, and a couple of tunny boats. We'll use it as a base."

"You'll need a front," Langley said.

I nodded. "That's where you come in. I want a permit to allow archaeological diving in that bay which you'll probably have to get from the Libyan Embassy in Rome. Stavrou will have to pull a few strings. I shouldn't imagine it's beyond him."

"What are we supposed to be looking for?" Angelo asked.

"A Roman wreck," I said. "That should sound well enough. The whole area's stiff with them anyway."

"Which means diving equipment," Barzini said. "No trouble there. There's plenty on board *Palmyra* now."

"More than that. I want three or four Roman wine jars. You know the sort of thing. Typical amphorae that have been lying on the seabed for sixteen or seventeen hundred years. Preferably encrusted with seashells. I hear the fishermen bring them up in their trawl nets off Marsala all the time."

"They're even selling them in the antique shops now to tourists," Barzini said.

"We'll also need Libyan army uniforms and they get their hardware from Russia these days which means AK assault rifles." He started to smile and I said, "Yes, I know, by a strange coincidence you just happen to have a warehouse full of them. Where are they bound for—Belfast or Bahrein?"

Langley said, "When do you intend to go?"

"If we miss this coming Friday, we'll have to wait another week," I said. "And that could be fatal. It's Monday now. Could we get together what we need and have the boat down at Capo Passero by Wednesday morning?"

"I don't see why not," Barzini said.

I said to Langley, "Which means that weather permitting, we could be in Gela Thursday night."

"Always supposing everything goes according to plan," he said.

I shrugged. "That's what makes life exciting. You'd better get back to Stavrou first thing in the morning. Fill him in on all this and get Zingari on the first flight out to Tripoli and tell him to be waiting at Gela Thursday night."

"What about you?"

"I've got things to do here. I'll be down with the boat."

I think he was going to argue, but Angelo cut in impatiently. "Can I go now?"

"Okay, okay," Barzini said. "Go and knock hell out of her, but be back here at eight or I'll have your ears."

Angelo departed. Nino, incredibly, was snoring in a chair in the corner. Barzini threw up his hands in despair. "I ask you, what can you do with them." His face brightened as if at a sudden thought. "Heh, I got something that might interest you, Oliver. A new gun. I'll show you."

He took out a key on the end of his watchchain and unlocked a small door in the corner. He switched on a light and we followed him down some wooden steps to a long whitewashed corridor.

He flicked another switch illuminating a row of targets at the far end each representing a charging soldier of indeterminate nationality, then opened a drawer in a table by the wall and took out a tin box. Whatever was stencilled on it was in Russian.

"A Stechkin," he said. "A true machine pistol. Best I've seen since the Mauser. Better than the Browning in every department. You can actually fire this baby on fully automatic if you want to."

As I opened the box, Langley moved to join me. The Stechkin was in a wooden holster and when I took it out I saw that it was similar to the Browning in appearance at least.

"Five inch barrel, twenty round magazine," Barzini said. "A hell of a lot of gun, especially if you use the wooden holster as a stock. They tell me a good shot can consistently hit a man-size target at up to a hundred and fifty yards."

"Now there's a challenge, if you like," Langley said. "May I, old stick?"

He hefted the Stechkin first in his right then in his left and finally tried it both hands together.

Barzini passed him an ammunition clip. "The safety selector's on the left behind the slide. Semiautomatic in the center, automatic at the top."

Langley took careful aim and shot the first target through the head, then he fired five times rapidly and scored five hits in the heart area, three close together, the other two straying towards the edge.

"Not bad," he said, "but I think the trigger needs lightening."

He went on to automatic and shredded the second target with what was left in the magazine. He turned and handed the weapon to me without a word.

Barzini gave me another magazine and I reloaded, took aim and fired half a dozen times at the third target. I nicked the edge of the heart once and the rest were in the shoulder area except for one which seemed to have missed altogether.

Langley shook his head. "It just isn't your day, is it? Ah, well, I suppose I'd better wend my way."

He started for the door and Barzini said, "Heh, smart boy, aren't you forgetting something?"

Langley smiled, took the envelope from his inside breast pocket and threw it on the table. "I thought you'd never ask. I'll be seeing you, old stick."

He went up the steps whistling softly between his teeth. The door closed behind him. Barzini took out the bank draft and examined it.

I said, "I'd cash it first thing in the morning if I were you."

"Tell me," he said. "The business earlier in the car about being too old and now this? Letting Langley make a fool of you."

"So he thinks he has an edge." I shrugged. "What harm does it do if it makes him feel good."

I fired three times so rapidly that to anyone except an expert it must have sounded like one shot, putting a bullet between the eyes of each of the remaining targets.

I put the Stechkin down on the table and nodded, "Yes, that really is a most remarkable weapon. Remind me to take one along, will you?"

I moved past him and went up the stairs.

CHAPTER SIX

THE RULES OF
THE GAME

WE CAME INTO THE HORSESHOE BAY below the villa at Capo Passero just before noon on Wednesday. Having left Palermo at midnight, we'd had an excellent passage, taking the western route past Marsala through the Sicilian Channel and the Golfo di Gela.

The Cessna was moored to the two buoys in the center of the bay and as we moved in towards the stone jetty the Landrover came down the dirt road which hardly surprised me. I suppose we must have been under scrutiny from the ramparts for quite some time.

Barzini was in the wheelhouse and Nino and Angelo fended the *Palmyra* off as we bumped against the jetty and I went over the rail with a line. As I looped it round a bollard, Langley got out of the Landrover followed by Gatano and came toward me.

"Hello there, old stick. How's every little thing?"

Gatano's face was badly bruised and there were stitches in the left cheek, the whole combining to make him look uglier than ever.

"Who's your friend?" I asked.

Gatano was holding a Sterling sub-machine gun and the look on his face was such that for a moment I thought he might be tempted to use it.

"Still full of the joys of spring, I see," Langley said. "The old man wants to see you and Barzini. The others can stay here."

"Anything to oblige." I turned to look up at Barzini as he cut the engine and leaned out of the wheelhouse window. "Royal command, Aldo. We're going visiting."

"That's nice," he said and came out on deck.

He was wearing a Smith and Wesson .38 in a spring holster on his left hip, butt forward. Langley said, "You leave that down here."

Barzini shrugged, took the gun out of the holster, leaned inside the wheelhouse and dropped it on the chart table. Langley turned to me. "What about you?"

I raised my hands without a word. He searched me anyway, completely missing a favorite place for a concealed weapon in expert opinion—the small of the back tucked into the pants under the shirt. Not that I'd anything there this time as it happened, but it was a serious flaw and certainly gave me pause for thought where Langley was concerned.

He slipped back, apparently satisfied. "All right, old stick, let's go."

Gatano stayed on the jetty, sitting on a bollard, the Sterling across his knees. Barzini and I got into the rear of the Landrover and Langley took the wheel.

"How's my sister?" I asked him as we drove away.

"Fine, old stick." He smiled with what appeared to be genuine warmth. "Lovely girl. Practices the piano most of the day. Perfectly happy. And Simone's been spending some time with her."

"Plus Frau Kubel and her Doberman?" I said. "How nice. All we need to make up the party is Charles Lutwidge Dodgson and we're all set for an idyllic afternoon on the river."

"Dodgson?" Barzini looked puzzled. "Who in the hell is this Dodgson?"

"Better known as Lewis Carroll. *Alice in Wonderland* and all that," Langley said. "Not to worry. Our friend's feeling a little pensive this morning, that's all."

He braked to a halt in the courtyard; we got out and started up through the garden to the high terrace. Stavrou was standing at the wall peering down into the bay. For a moment there was a fugue in time and I was conscious of an irrational coldness. It was as if nothing had happened—as if it were still that first day when they'd brought me up from the Hole. The table laid for lunch, the bottles of *Zibibbo* in the bucket, the waiter at the ready, Moro and Bonetti in the same fisherman jerseys standing stolidly side by side, arms folded.

Stavrou swung around and looked at us. "So this is Mr. Barzini?" he said. "A well-found ship, sir. I congratulate you."

He lurched forward on his two sticks and the waiter eased him into the chair then poured him a glass of wine. He sampled some with a sigh of content and looked up at me.

"Well, sir, and how does it go?"

"I want to see my sister," I said. "Before anything else."

He nodded to Langley without the slightest hesitation. "All right, Justin. Five minutes."

Langley moved through the archway into the garden beyond and I went after him. This time there was no music playing, but I could hear laughter and a dog barked.

We paused by a small wall and looked down into a sunken garden. Hannah was seated on the ground on a rug, Simone beside her. She was throwing a rubber ball for the Doberman, who chased it eagerly and brought it back to her each time. Frau Kubel sat on a stone bench, knitting.

"Strange how that dog has taken to her," Langley said. "I just can't understand it."

Simone glanced up and saw us. The smile left her face and she stood. I heard Hannah quite distinctly ask her what was wrong.

Langley tugged at my sleeve. "All right, old stick. Better get back now. We don't want to upset him, do we?"

There didn't seem much I could say to that so I turned and led the way back to the high terrace where we found Stavrou and Barzini with their heads together over a British Admiralty chart for the Libyan coastline, Cap Bon to Tobruk.

Stavrou looked up. "Ah, there you are. Now you can tell me all about it."

"You got the permit from the Libyan Embassy for archaeological diving?" I asked.

Langley produced a large buff envelope from which he took out an imposing document with no less than four wax seals on it.

"This cost money," he said. "So watch it."

I leaned over the chart. "If we leave this evening we can be in Gela the same time on Thursday. All I need then is Zingari. If he lets us down we're finished."

"He won't," Stavrou said. "I'm paying him too much, but tell me everything from the beginning."

"All right. We sail into Gela posing as underwater archaeologists looking for a Roman wreck in the bay. We've got several amphorae with us which can go over the side under cover of darkness to be publicly recovered for the whole village to see the following day. That should keep everyone happy."

"And the assault on the prison?" Stavrou said. "What takes place there?"

"I presume Langley has told you about Angelo Carter?" Stavrou nodded and I carried on, "He gains access to the prison as indicated. Once inside his one aim is to get to the north wall and dispose of the two sentries there."

"That seems one hell of a tall order to me."

"But not to Carter. He was a Green Beret. He has a light line with him which he drops down. I'll be waiting on the rocks at the base of the cliff with Nino Barzini. We attach a climbing rope to the line, which Carter hauls up. Then Nino, who's an expert in these matters, climbs it, drops a body line to me and he and Carter haul me up between them."

"All right, supposing all that works."

"Carter changes, then we cross quite openly to the Commandant's house, passing ourselves off as soldiers. Colonel Masmoudi has a weakness for the ladies which means he tends to be very fully occupied on a Friday night. We shouldn't have too much trouble in overpowering him."

"Then what happens?"

"He does as he's told like a good boy and has your stepson brought to his house. Then we all leave by the front gate nice and quietly in Masmoudi's car. Drive straight to Gela and embark. At that time of night the tunny boats are out in force about ten miles off shore. One or two nets draped from our mast is all we need and we'll be lost in the crowd."

There was a lengthy silence while Stavrou looked at the map. I helped myself to *Zibibbo*. Finally, he turned to Barzini. "What do you think?"

"I'm going, aren't I?" Barzini pointed out.

"I don't know." Stavrou shook his head. "There are too many ifs."

"You're right," Barzini said cheerfully. "The plain truth is that if everything falls right for us, we can't fail, but if even one single item goes wrong then the whole house of cards comes tumbling down."

Stavrou nodded, looking at the map. "Justin has a point to make."

"And what might that be?" I said.

Langley grinned. "You're not going to like this, old stick, but it's a fact. Imagine you're walking across the courtyard of the prison wearing Libyan uniforms, making straight for Masmoudi's house."

"So what?"

"What happens when the sergeant of the guard or an officer, or even just a stray soldier calls out good night or asks you what you're doing?"

"Simple," Barzini said. "I'd say I'm on a special detail for the colonel."

"Oh, I see," Langley said. "I didn't realize you spoke Arabic."

There was a heavy silence and I said, "That's what's called not seeing the wood for the trees."

"You mean you don't speak Arabic either, old stick?" Langley said. "Never mind. I do."

Which was what the whole damned thing had been leading up to, of course. I saw it all now, just as I saw with equal certainty, that he was right.

"Okay," I said. "Welcome aboard." I turned to Stavrou. "Happy now?"

He smiled delightedly. "That's what I like about you, sir. You're a sport."

"Who's hot and thirsty and badly in need of a shower," I said. "Which is exactly what I'm now going to have," and I left them there and moved up through the garden to my room.

I took my time over the shower, going over the whole thing in my mind Stavrou was right—there were too many ifs, but I couldn't help that any more than I could help the business with Langley. He was right there also. The inability to make some sort of response in Arabic if required was just the sort of detail on which the whole thing could fail. Most Libyans spoke Italian, that was true, a relic of Mussolini's dreams of Empire, but not among themselves.

So, Langley would have to go, as Stavrou had obviously intended all along, to keep a watching brief. I didn't like the idea, but it was something we'd have to put up with.

I pulled on a bathrobe and went out into the living room towelling my hair. Simone was sitting on the terrace gazing out to sea. She didn't turn round so I draped the towel around my neck, went to the drinks trolley and mixed two large gin and tonics.

I put one on the wall in front of her and took the other chair. "Well?" I said.

She turned her head slowly to look at me. Her face was as calm, as enigmatic as usual, but there was something in the eyes. Some kind of personal hurt.

She said, with a kind of anger, "What do you expect me to do?"

"I don't expect you to do anything."

She picked up the gin and tonic, swallowed about half of it, then sat staring down into the glass, holding it in both hands. When she spoke it was obviously with great difficulty.

"Your sister—she's a nice person."

"I would have thought I'd made that plain enough to you a long time ago."

Somewhere not too far away, Hannah started to play. Ravel—*Pavane on the death of an Infanta*. Infinitely beautiful in the still heat of the garden, touching something deep inside. Life itself, perhaps at the very center of things.

She was crying now, slow, heavy tears, and when she spoke her voice was hoarse and broken. "I suppose what I'm really trying to say is that I'm sorry."

"Who for? Me, Hannah, or yourself?"

It was brutal enough, I suppose, but she took it well. Strange, but I was almost proud of her when she tilted her chin bravely and looked me straight in the face.

"All right, Oliver, I deserved that, but I'm not going to crawl. I've crawled enough in my time." She stood up. "I hear Justin is going with you."

"That's right."

"Watch him—there's more to this thing than you think."

Which didn't exactly surprise me. I said, "What, for instance?"

She certainly put on a good show of distress and uncertainty. "I don't know, I really don't, but there's something. I just wanted you to know that."

"All right," I said. "You've told me."

And now she was angry again, much more the old Simone I'd known and loved. The glass went sailing over the wall into space. "You bastard," she said, turned and walked rapidly away.

I sat there finishing my drink and thinking about what she'd said, and Barzini appeared. "Langley said I'd find you up here. Heh, I just passed a very angry young woman. When I asked her if I was on the right track for you she told me to go to hell."

"It's not one of her good days." I went back inside to the bedroom and started to dress.

Barzini leaned in the doorway. "Stavrou wants us to have lunch with him. Afterwards he'd like to look over *the Palmyra*."

"He can wait," I said. "I've more important things on my mind. The way things have turned out, Langley's going to be breathing down our necks from now on and I want a chance to talk to Nino and Angelo Carter alone while there's still time."

"And just how do we do that?"

I grinned. "Just stick with me. To the pure in heart all things are possible."

I moved out on to the terrace, Barzini at my heels, and took one of the back paths down through the garden, avoiding the high terrace where Stavrou was waiting.

The Landrover was standing in the courtyard, the gate was open and no one appeared to be around. Barzini scrambled into the passenger seat and I got behind the wheel. As we moved out through the gateway, Bonetti ran out of the garage shouting, but by then it was too late.

I drove very rapidly down the dirt road and pulled up on the jetty beside *Palmyra*. Nino and Angelo were lounging in the stern smoking and talking. Gatano was sitting in the prow, the sub-machine gun across his knees.

He stood up, scowling, as I jumped down on deck followed by Barzini. "Heh, what is this? Where's Mr. Langley?"

"Oh, he'll be along," I said. "Any minute now."

I crowded straight into him before he knew what was happening, close enough to get a grip on his shirt, turned my thigh in a simple hip throw that bounced him against the rail. He hung precariously for a moment and then went over, sub-machine gun and all.

We left him floundering and joined Nino and Angelo who were sitting up and taking notice. I squatted in front of them and Barzini said, "You haven't got long. Langley's coming."

I glanced up and saw a Mercedes on its way down and already at the turn in the dirt road. Nino said, "What is this?"

"I wanted a private word, that's all," I said. "There's been a slight change of plan. Langley's joining the team, apparently for the general good, but I'm not so sure about that. There's something else going on here—something a whole lot deeper, so watch him every minute of the day and night. He's the original slippery fish."

"He doesn't look much to me," Angelo observed.

"That's exactly what twenty-one men said about Billy the Kid," I told him. "And look where it got them."

Gatano floundered out of the shallows to the beach and the Mercedes turned onto the jetty and braked to a halt. Langley got out and Moro followed him clutching a Sterling.

Langley seemed amused. He watched Gatano make it to the end of the jetty then looked down at the rest of us. "What was all that about?"

"I bumped into him," I said. "Sheer accident."

"I'm sure it was. Anyway, if you've said what it is you didn't want me to hear, Mr. Stavrou would be pleased to see all of you up on the high terrace for lunch."

Gatano chose that precise moment to arrive at a shambling trot, those great hands of his ready to grab at my throat. Langley tripped him deftly, Gatano went sprawling. He tried to get up, sobbing with rage and Langley put a foot on his left hand.

"That's all—understand?"

Gatano looked up at him, eyes glazed, and then he subsided like a hurt dog.

"You'd think he'd have had enough by now," I said.

"Ah, but then some people never learn, do they, old stick?" He smiled beautifully. "Now, if you'd like to join me in the Merc, the others can follow in the Landrover."

Which I did. When I looked down at the turn in the dirt road, Gatano was on his own, walking.

The meal was pretty much a repetition of the one I'd had with Stavrou and Simone on that first night Once again he drank a great deal of wine, ate huge quantities of food and talked incessantly on every subject under the sun.

There was no sign of Simone who, I presumed, was with Hannah, but in any event Stavrou made no mention of her. When the meal was finished he announced his intention of looking over the boat although it was obvious to everyone there that he couldn't even negotiate the companionway.

Langley took him down in the Mercedes and the rest of us followed in the Landrover. He actually did get out, but conducted his inspection from the quayside, discussing the *Palmyra* with Barzini in a considerable amount of technical detail, showing a surprising knowledge of small sea-going craft in general.

Langley finally took him away and we got on with our final equipment check. Barzini went through the list with Nino, then I did the whole thing again, helped by Angelo Carter, just to make sure.

Finally, Barzini and I had a look at the charts in the wheelhouse while Nino and Angelo topped up the tanks from four fifty-gallon drums we'd carried as deck cargo.

"What do you think?" I said.

"We should be all right. I got the weather report on the radio. Three to four wind. Rain squalls. It might blow a little harder before morning, but nothing to get worried about." He chuckled. "Maybe enough to keep this Langley with his face in a bucket."

"You don't like him?"

"Half a man," he said contemptuously. "What is there left to like?" He stuck one of those vile Egyptian cheroots in his mouth. "And this Stavrou." He shook his head. "It must have been a very large stone, but underneath one is where they found him."

Nino called, "Someone coming."

The Landrover came down the dirt road and paused at the end of the jetty. Simone got out, wearing a straw hat, dark glasses, and a bikini and carrying a large beach bag. She glanced towards us briefly, then started down to the shore, and the Landrover moved on.

Langley got out and stood at the edge of the jetty. "Ready for off, are we?"

"Just about," I said.

"Mr. Stavrou would like a word before you go—with all of you."

Behind him, Simone dived off a rock and started to swim out into the bay in a fast, powerful crawl. There was little point in arguing, so I nodded to the others, who were standing listening to the conversation, and everyone got into the Landrover again.

Stavrou was waiting on the high terrace, seated at the table. This time the bottles in the bucket were champagne. The waiter filled glasses quickly and brought them round on a silver tray. He even wore white gloves.

Stavrou raised his glass. "A toast, gentlemen. Fair winds and good fortune."

The whole thing was getting more farcical by the minute. I said, "Can we go now? I'd like to get started."

"Time for another glass, sir, and I'd like a word in your private ear before you leave." He pushed himself up, balancing on the sticks. "Your friend may join us if he wishes. He may find what I have to say of some interest"

He moved to the parapet, Langley carrying his champagne for him and Barzini and I followed. Langley handed him the glass and Stavrou looked over the ramparts. "A long way down, gentlemen."

Nobody made any comment. We all waited and after a while he said, "You are familiar with Greek mythology, Major Grant?"

"Get to the point," I told him.

77

"I'm thinking particularly of the Theseus legend. When he returned from Crete his crew hoisted black sails, the signal of ill-success, in error and Aegeus the King, thinking his son dead, threw himself into the sea."

There was a heavy silence and even Langley wasn't smiling. Stavrou said softly, "When you are sighted on your return, Major Grant, I shall be waiting up here on the high terrace with your sister and I will expect to see my son on deck as you enter the bay. If not, then I regret to say that history, in a manner of speaking, will repeat itself."

I fought for breath, schooling myself to stillness, fighting to keep my hands off him, for there was no purpose to be served in that—not now. When I finally spoke I was surprised at my own calmness.

"You've got a clump of bamboo down by the fountain that reminds me of Vietnam. The Viet Cong were rather partial to a lethal little item called a *punji* stick. Sharpened bamboo stuck in the ground smeared with excrement. A nasty festering wound if you stepped on one. I once saw a marine who'd been tied down across half a dozen of them and he'd taken a long time to die. Now I'll do this job for you. I'll try and get your bloody stepson out, but you harm my sister in any way and you know what you get, my word on it."

His eyes were very dark, the face white. Strangely enough it was Langley who tugged at my sleeve and said quietly, "I think we should go now, old stick."

I turned on my heel and went down through the garden without another word and the others followed. We all got into the Landrover and Moro took us down to the jetty. There was no sign of Simone, not that it mattered, for reaction was setting in and I was filled with a blank, despairing, killing rage. I stumbled going over the rail and when Barzini took my arm I started to shake.

"I'll kill him! I'll kill the bastard!" I said hoarsely.

"We'll go now," Barzini said firmly. "Take the wheel."

He was right, of course, for at least it gave my hands something to do. I went into the wheelhouse and pressed the starter, the engines picking up instantly. Nino and Angelo cast off, I took *Palmyra* round past the Cessna in a long sweeping curve and headed out to sea.

CHAPTER SEVEN

DEAD ON COURSE

I TOOK THE FIRST WATCH AND nobody argued, mainly because I was fit company for no man in that mood. Dusk was falling now, and I switched on the navigation lights and checked my course.

I stood there in the gathering darkness staring out to sea, crushed by guilt for the moment. The consequences, if I failed, were terrible to contemplate and it was all my fault for if I had not been the man I was, led the sort of life I had done, Hannah would not have been touched by any of this.

The masthead light swung rhythmically from side to side and spray scattered across the window. A couple of points to starboard the red and green navigation lights of a steamer were clearly visible. It had its own kind of peace, all this. I felt a little calmer, put her on automatic pilot and sat back in the swivel seat to light a cigarette.

I reached under the chart table and released a spring catch. A flap fell down which held a Stechkin machine pistol in spring clips, a slight improvement Barzini and I had fitted up together the previous evening when Nino and Angelo weren't around.

The door clicked open behind me. I tried to close the flap, too late, and Simone said, "Very neat, but then you always did like to be prepared for any and every possibility."

I said, "What's the story?"

"I waited until you'd all gone up to the villa, then came on board and hid in the engine room," she said. "I had clothes in my beach bag."

"All right—why?"

"Because I couldn't stand being with Stavrou anymore. Because I love you."

"Am I supposed to feel flattered?"

There was a short pause and then she moved forward so that I could see her face disembodied in the light from the compass.

"Not really. But that's what I was told to say." She moved very close now, sliding her arms about my neck, pushing those good breasts against me. "I'm also supposed to prove it in every possible way."

I put my hands on her waist which seemed the natural thing to do. "Stavrou sent you?"

"That's right."

"Does Langley know?"

"Of course."

"I see. You're supposed to help him out. Pass on any useful information and so forth?" I put my hand under the chart table and dropped the flap again. "You could tell him about this for a start."

"I suppose I could." Her lips brushed against my right ear. "I'm sure of one thing. Langley's up to something. I don't know what, but it's a fact of life."

"Why should I trust you now? I tried it once, remember."

"I know," she said. "So you'll just have to chance your arm because what we're talking about now isn't me or you, but your sister." She pulled away slightly. "Whether you believe this or not doesn't really matter, but the first thing I knew about her involvement was when Justin flew her in from Palermo."

"All right," I said. "A change of heart. We'll see." I closed the flap under the chart table, reached up to the bulkhead and dropped another one down containing an Israeli Uzi sub-machine gun.

"Tell him about that one. He'll think you're nicely on the ball."

"All right."

She stayed close to me, her right leg trapped between my knees. I flicked the intercom switch and pressed the buzzer. Barzini said, "What's up?"

"Better get up here," I said. "And bring Langley with you. We're carrying excess cargo."

They were with us in a few moments, Barzini leading the way. He pulled up short when he saw Simone. "What's all this?"

"She's decided to change sides, that's all," I said.

Langley certainly put on an excellent show. "Why, you stupid little bitch," he said. "Stavrou will have your hide for this."

He reached for her and I knocked his arm away. "She's with me from now on, so hands off. I'll sort it out with Stavrou when we get back."

Langley laughed shortly. "Suit yourself, old stick, and much good may it do you. I mean, she has rather been passed from hand to hand. Did she tell you about that whorehouse she worked at in Paris, by the way? All sorts of peculiar goings on there, I can tell you."

She lunged at him and Barzini got in the way. Langley moved out while the going was good, laughing delightedly and Barzini leaned against the door to stop the girl following him.

Simone turned, furiously angry. I said, "I'm damned if I know who put up the better performance. You or Langley."

"What do I have to do to convince you?" She slapped me across the face. "Cut off my right hand?" For the first time there was a hint of genuine distress in her voice. "All right, Oliver, maybe I've spent too much time at gutter level, but you've been there yourself."

"Okay," I said. "If it makes you feel better, I believe you. Take her below, Aldo, and put Nino and Carter in the picture."

He opened the door for her. As she turned to go I added, "Don't forget to tell him about the submachine gun. His reaction might prove interesting."

They left me and I sat there thinking about things for a while. Not that there was any solution, not at that time, so I unlocked the automatic steering, altered course a point to starboard and sat there, hands on the wheel as *Palmyra* plowed on into the night.

Barzini reappeared after a couple of hours with a mug of coffee. "You get some rest now. I'll take over for a while."

"All right," I said.

He moved past me to take the wheel and I gave him the course. He said, "What in the hell goes on?"

"I haven't the slightest idea. The only thing I'm certain of is that Stavrou hasn't told us everything. That's why Langley was slipped in at the last moment. If it hadn't been for the Arabic thing they'd have come up with some equally valid excuse."

"What about the girl?"

I put him in the picture there. Told him everything including the bit about the Uzi in the bulkhead flap.

"I see," he said. "You think if she tells him about that he'll think she's doing a good job?"

"Something like that."

"Can we trust her?"

"I don't know. She knows about the Stechkin as well, remember."

"I see. She tells him about the Uzi, but doesn't tell him about the Stechkin, means she's on our side?" He shook his head. "How will you know? Langley wouldn't be fool enough to take them. Not at this stage of the game."

"Exactly, so we wait and see. I'm going to get some sleep now. Wake me in three hours and I'll take another turn at the wheel."

I opened the door, moved along the heaving deck, head down against the rain and went below.

I slept in the aft cabin and when I awakened it was almost three o'clock. Simone was fast asleep on the other bunk covered by a blanket, her face calm and untroubled.

Nino and Angelo, I knew, were bunking forward and when I went into the saloon, Langley was lying on one of the bench seats. He seemed to be asleep although I couldn't be sure. Not that it mattered and I went up the companionway softly.

There was quite a sea and cold spray stung my face as I moved along the deck and opened the wheelhouse door. Barzini was standing at the wheel, a cheroot between his teeth. The smell was terrible and I opened a window.

"Don't say it," he told me cheerfully. "I don't know how I stand it myself."

"Years of practice," I said. "What's the situation?"

"Dead on course and making good time. There's been a sea running for about half an hour now. Nothing to worry about. I tried getting a weather report, but there was too much radio interference. Electric storm somewhere out there."

Lightning flickered on the horizon. I eased past him and took the wheel. "I'll spell you again in three or four hours," he said and went out.

I sat there feeling the wheel kick in my hands and outside the wind scattered the rain in silver cobwebs through the navigation lights. It was all rather pleasant. The world, the outside world, in a manner of speaking, had ceased to exist.

It was perhaps a couple of hours later that the door opened softly and Simone came in with a tray. I could smell coffee and something more. The delicious scent of fried bacon.

"Now what are you trying to do, spoil me?"

She put the tray down on the chart table, pulled out a stool and sat down. I helped myself to one of the bacon sandwiches. "I hear you and Langley had your heads together earlier."

"That's right."

"Did you mention the Uzi?"

She nodded. "I told him that I saw you checking it through the window of the wheelhouse."

"And what did he have to say to that?"

"Nothing much." She shrugged. "He said he'd take care of it and told me to keep my eyes open for anything else out of the ordinary."

There was a light on the horizon to starboard.

"What's that?" she asked.

"Malta," I said. "St. George's Head light."

"And how far have we to go?"

"From our starting point to Cape Misratah on the Libyan coast is about three hundred and twenty miles."

I think she'd asked the question more for something to say than anything else. For a while she sat there in silence while I finished the sandwiches and then said with some slight hesitation, "If you don't mind, I'd like to ask you something."

"All right," I said. "Fire away."

"I read the file Stavrou has on you. Some of the things you did when you were an Intelligence Officer were incredible, but afterward..."

"There was only one difference," I said. "Afterward I did it for rather large sums of money."

She said fiercely, "I don't understand. There was no need. With your background, your intelligence, there wasn't a single thing you couldn't have done if you'd wanted to. Instead ..."

"I turned thief," I said. "To put it in simple and honest terms."

"But why? I don't understand."

"Because I enjoyed it."

"I don't believe you."

"Why not? The kind of intelligence work I did for the army before I was kicked out was simply criminal behavior made legal and I happen to have a flair for that sort of thing."

"You ruined yourself." There was a note of genuine concern in her voice. "What you did for that student who was in trouble in Czechoslovakia was magnificent, but the other things." She shook her head. "You threw everything away. Career, reputation, and for what?"

"Money," I said. "Lots of it. On top of that I've enjoyed it. Every golden moment."

She went out angrily without another word, banging the door. I didn't have much time to consider what she'd said because right about then it started to blow, hail rattling against the windshield like lead bullets.

I checked the chart again, then altered course a couple of points and increased speed, racing the heavy weather and the waves grew rougher, rocking the *Palmyra* from side to side.

The door opened in a flurry of rain and Barzini came in wearing a yellow oilskin. "So, it starts!"

"Likely to get worse before it gets better," I said.

He looked pleased at the prospect, but then he always had been more at home with a deck under his feet than a pavement. "Good, I'll take over for a while. You get some more sleep."

I didn't argue, gave him the wheel, negotiated the heaving deck, not without some difficulty, and went below.

Langley was still sleeping, or apparently sleeping, in the saloon, but there was no sign of Simone when I went into the aft cabin. Presumably she was in the galley, not that I intended to lose any sleep over it because I was suddenly rather tired. I closed my eyes and opened them again, apparently in the same moment, to find her shaking me gently.

"What time is it?" I asked.

"Almost two o'clock. You've slept about seven hours. Mr. Barzini told me to leave you."

Gray light streamed in through the port hole above the bunk and waves slapped against the hull with a sullen angry sound. I followed her out into the saloon and found Barzini seated at the table eating ham and eggs.

He grinned. "Heh, she can cook, this girl."

He slipped an arm around her waist. She said to me, "See, I'm appreciated by someone."

"That must make you feel warm all over," I said. "If you can spare the time, I'll have the same."

She went into the galley and I helped myself to coffee. "Who's got the wheel?"

"Langley," Barzini said.

I frowned. "What about Nino and Carter?"

"See for yourself."

I opened the door of the forrard cabin and the smell told me everything I needed to know before I looked in. Nino was sitting on the edge of a bunk with a plastic bucket between his knees and Angelo Carter was flat on his back groaning loudly.

I closed the door. "Not so good."

"Men of straw," Barzini said.

I watched him shoveling in the ham and eggs and suddenly my own appetite seemed to have waned considerably. I put down the coffee and reached for an oilskin.

"Tell Simone I changed my mind. I'll go topside and see how Langley is doing."

The sea really was running now and cold rain lashed my face as I went along the heaving deck to the wheelhouse. Langley was standing at the wheel, a cigarette in his mouth.

"Ah, there you are, old stick. Anything to eat down there?"

"I should imagine so." I took over the wheel and he moved out of the way. "How's it going?"

"Pretty fair. I just checked the weather on the radio. Wind force seven—heavy squalls—rain. Moderating towards evening. How are Nino and Carter?"

"Flat on their backs."

He grinned. "Ah, well, some of us have it and some of us don't, I suppose. See you later, old stick," and he opened the door and went out.

The wheel kicked like a living thing and the seas grew rougher, rocking *Palmyra* violently and once again I tried increasing speed until the prow seemed to reach clean out of the water each time a wave rolled beneath her.

It was an exhilarating experience and for the next hour, I was totally involved in the task in hand. Finally, Barzini appeared.

"I'll take over," he said. "Go and have a cup of coffee."

As I was about to go out, I suddenly remembered the Uzi sub-machine gun. Langley had certainly been up here on his own for long enough to do something about it if he wanted to.

I pulled down the flap and Barzini glanced up. "Still there. Did the girl tell him?"

"So she says."

I took the Uzi down and weighed it in my hands for a moment. Everything seemed perfectly normal. I took out the ammunition clip, checked it and replaced it, which seemed to be that. I was about to put it back when something made me look at the firing pin— instinct, I suppose. It was a good job that I did because the end had been nipped off, probably with a pair of pliers.

I showed Barzini. "The bastard," he said angrily and dropped the flap under the chart table and got the Stechkin.

I checked it over thoroughly, but everything seemed to be in perfect working order. I replaced them both and Barzini said, "So, the girl was telling the truth. She is on your side."

"I'll reserve judgment on that one."

"What about this other business? Are you going to confront Langley?"

"No point," I said. "For the time being it's enough that we know."

I went below feeling unaccountably cheerful. Certainly in the right mood for ham and eggs this time. Langley, having eaten, had taken Simone's bunk in the aft cabin and appeared to be sleeping.

Simone gave me my meal and left me to go up on deck. I went up again myself when I'd finished eating and found her in the wheelhouse with Barzini. She turned to greet me excitedly as I opened the door.

"We're there, Oliver! We're there!"

Something of an exaggeration, but on the other hand, there was no doubt that the gray smudge on the horizon, visible now and then through the curtain of rain, was the coast of Libya, Cape Misratah, to be precise.

CHAPTER EIGHT

FIRE IN THE NIGHT

IN SPITE OF THE WEATHER WE sighted a considerable number of small fishing craft on the way in—tunny boats mostly. By the time we were close inshore, the storm seemed to have blown itself out, the wind dropping, leaving only a calm gray evening with a light rain falling.

The entrance to Gela Bay was a narrow passage between two jagged peaks which according to the charts, were known as the Sisters. Inside, there was an enormous landlocked lagoon fringed by white beaches and backed by a scattering of palm trees. There was a stone pier and a couple of motorized fishing dhows were tied up there. There were perhaps half-a-dozen flat-roofed houses scattered among the palm trees—no more.

We dropped anchor in a part of the channel where there was eight to ten fathoms of water. Barzini cut the engine and came out to join Langley and Simone and me at the rail.

The rain hissed down into the water of the lagoon. "Come to sunny Africa," Langley observed.

"So what?" I said. "You're not here to get a tan."

Nino and Angelo Carter appeared from the companionway looking pale. I said to Simone, "Try to get some food down them, will you? We've got work to do. They aren't going to be much good in this state."

She shepherded them below and Barzini said, "Now what?"

"I'll go ashore and see what's what. Zingari might be there now. You never know. Are you coming?"

"No, I'll stay. Take the pretty boy here with you. He probably needs the exercise."

If he was trying to bait Langley he was wasting his time for he simply grinned good-humoredly and gave me a hand to get the large inflatable dinghy over the side.

I pressed the starting button on the outboard motor and we moved in toward the shore. There wasn't much activity. An Arab with a white turban wound around his head, came out of the wheelhouse of one of the fishing boats and looked across at us and a small boy stood at the water's edge in the rain and watched us come in.

We ran the dinghy up on shore and got out. Langley said, "Now what?"

"I don't know," I said. "Maybe Zingari won't be here until later. We'll have a look around."

"At what?" he inquired.

I led the way, moving up from the beach past the stone pier. The houses were poor places, two of them on the edge of an olive grove. Another had a large veranda and, to judge by the baskets and fishing nets which hung from the roof and the cooking pots on display, was obviously the local store.

A man wearing a woolen *barracan,* the day-to-day dress of the average Libyan, was drinking a bottle of beer and watching us at the same time.

At the other end of the olive grove there was a huddle of black goatskin tents, a hobbled gray camel and a few goats grazing on the stunted grass. Nothing else except the harsh, barren landscape beyond, the dirt road dwindling into infinity.

"What do you think?" Langley said.

"We'll have a beer. If he doesn't come soon we'll go back to the *Palmyra* and wait there."

The man in the *barracan* on the veranda of the store came down the steps to greet us as we approached. "One of you gentlemen is Signor Grant?" he said in excellent Italian.

"That's me," I told him.

He smiled delightedly and showed us to a couple of cane chairs. "My good friend, Signor Zingari has been here this morning and told me to look out for you. He said he would be back this evening."

His name was Izmir and he owned the store and a half interest in a tunny boat or so he told us with the kind of cheerful lack of inhibition that some people show toward strangers.

He naturally wanted to know who we were. I told him we had a permit to dive in the area. That we were looking for old wrecks. I even offered to pay for any useful information he managed to obtain in that connection from local fishermen and he agreed enthusiastically.

He brought us a couple of bottles of warm beer, a local brew that was really quite pleasant and we'd just started drinking when an old Ford truck with a canvas tilt came over the rise by the olive grove and braked to a halt.

Zingari climbed down from behind the wheel. He was wearing the same shabby linen suit and straw hat and his face was paler, more anxious than ever and damp with sweat.

He patted his forehead with a grimy handkerchief and tried to smile as he came up the steps, "So, gentlemen, you are here."

"You look as cheerful as a man who's just learned he has about six months to live," Langley told him.

"A lifetime, signor, compared to how long I will live if anything goes wrong." He sat down, mopping away at his face. "This is a dangerous business. Colonel Masmoudi is a cruel man—the kind of man who delights in cruelty for its own sake. If you fell into his hands, gentlemen ..."

"But we won't," Langley said. "Positive thinking, my old dear, that's the order of the day."

Which didn't seem to have any appreciable effect on Zingari's morale. He swallowed some of the beer Izmir brought him.

"I'd like to take a look at the fortress," I said.

"You mean now?" His jaw sagged.

"Yes, from the sea. We'll go in the *Palmyra*. It shouldn't take long."

He looked distinctly unhappy. "But, signor, a boat nosing around in the area of Râs Kanai might arouse suspicion."

"A tunny boat?" I said. "With nets draped around the deck? I should have thought they must see dozens of those from up there on the ramparts."

He brightened at that—not too much, but enough to go inside to have a word with Izmir and when we went down to the dinghy a few minutes later we carried two large tunny nets between us.

The moment he was over the *Palmyra's* rail he darted into the wheelhouse as if for protection. Barzini was sitting on the engine-room hatch and stood up. "What's all that about?"

"Nothing," I said. "That's our good friend, Zingari. I thought we might take a little trip to see what the fort looks like from the sea and he's not exactly enchanted by the prospect."

"Holy Mother of God," Barzini said in disgust. "Sometimes I wonder how in the hell I ever allowed you to persuade me to join this crazy enterprise," and he went into the wheelhouse and pressed the button on the electric winch which immediately started to heave in the anchor.

Râs Kanai, Cape of Fear. It was well named. A grim, forbidding-looking place of jagged rocks and high cliffs and the fortress itself, half glimpsed through a drift of rain in the gathering darkness was quite something.

We'd draped nets from the mast down to the stern rail and I stood in their shelter and examined the situation through binoculars. The cliff below the south ramparts looked completely unclimbable to me and at their base, waves thundered in across a jumble of black rocks although there was also a narrow strip of shingle which promised some sort of toehold.

I passed the binoculars to Nino who kept them for only a few brief moments while he examined the cliff face. He gave them back to me and nodded cheerfully. "Nothing to it. Given time, I could get up there on my own. With a rope it will be a piece of cake."

"Even in darkness?"

"Most suitable time of all," he said. "Nothing to see if you look down."

Which seemed to take care of that so I handed the binoculars to Langley. He took rather longer over his inspection than Nino. "Two sentries," he said. "I can see them clearly enough. Nasty-looking cliffs those."

"You think you can get up them?" I said.

"Do you?"

I didn't seem to have a ready answer to that one. Certainly Simone looked serious enough and even Barzini wasn't smiling as he took *Palmyra* round in a wide circle and started back.

"Cheer up, Aldo." I leaned in the wheelhouse window and helped myself to one of his cheroots. " After all, you don't have to get up the damn thing, do you?"

Before he could reply, Zingari, who was standing in the corner by the door, looking if possible even more agitated than ever, cracked wide open.

"For pity's sake, Signor Grant, abandon this whole foolish scheme. No good will come of it."

Barzini said in disgust, "My God, and we're supposed to depend on that object."

Langley appeared in the open doorway. He stuck a cigarette in his mouth and scratched a match on the door. "What's the matter with you, then, old stick?" he said to Zingari. "Didn't Mr. Stavrou pay you enough?"

"Please—signor," Zingari protested. "Mr. Stavrou has been more than generous."

"Oh, I see. What you mean is that you didn't know what the job would entail before you took it."

Zingari oozed sweat, the little anguished eyes swivelled helplessly from side to side seeking escape where there was none.

Langley said, "Mr. Stavrou appreciates loyalty above most things. Last year, for example, he had dealings with a man called Cousceau in Algiers in connection with foreign exchange. Rather large sums were involved and friend Cousceau proved wanting."

Zingari licked dry lips. "Signor—please. What has this to do with me?"

"They found him in a cellar in the Casbah," Langley went on. "Nailed to a table. Hands and feet. He'd been there three days and he was certainly in no condition to get up and walk. You find this interesting?"

Zingari, face twitching in horror, seemed incapable of speech, which suited me just fine, for I was beginning to get the impression that the more scared Zingari was, the better it was for the rest of us.

We passed between the Sisters into the lagoon and dropped anchor again. It was almost dark and Zingari tugged at my sleeve as I stood at the rail.

"You need me anymore, Mr. Grant? Can I go now?"

"All right," I said. "Get in the boat."

I took him ashore myself, running the prow up onto the sand so that he could step out dry-footed. As he did so, I said, "Tomorrow morning."

He turned warily, bending to peer at my face through the darkness. "Signor?"

"Ten o'clock," I said. "Here, with the truck. I want you to show me everything. The prison, the road, Zabia. You understand me?"

"But Signor," he said, "there could be great danger in driving around in the immediate area of the prison. What if we are stopped?"

"I'm sure you'll think of something," I said. "Ten o'clock—and don't forget to let the customs authorities know we're here." I took the dinghy round and away, back toward *Palmyra*.

Everyone was in the saloon when I went down the companionway and Simone was pouring coffee. Nino and Angelo Carter seemed quite recovered and there was a reasonably cheerful atmosphere.

Barzini said, "He looks like a broken reed to me, that one. What do you think?"

"Langley put the fear of God into him," I said. "And I've just added a few coals to the fire. Let's hope it does the trick."

"And when do we have the dubious pleasure of his company again?" Langley inquired.

"Ten o'clock tomorrow," I said. "He's coming back with the truck to take me on a tour of inspection."

For once, there was no challenge in his voice. He was all business. "And who else?"

But I had already considered that question. "Angelo for one because he has to see the set-up at Zabia. One more, I think. You and Nino can argue about who."

He had a coin in his hand in a moment, nodded to Nino and tossed it. Nino called. Langley scooped up the coin with a grin. "All set then, old stick. You're stuck with me."

Which had a kind of inevitability about it, but I could worry about that later. "There's still one more chore to be done before knocking off for the night. I want those amphorae over the side."

"You expect visitors?" Barzini asked.

"I told Zingari to notify customs we're here when he gets back to Zabia. If they do turn up, I want the evidence that we're working away plain for all to see. First thing in the morning I'll go over the side and bring one back up in plain view of the beach. You or Nino can do the same later on in the morning when the rest of us are ashore. Go through the motions. Look busy."

The amphorae were in the forrard hold, great double-handled earthenware wine jars made to hold a good ten gallons each. Phoenician, Roman, Greek— they were found all over the eastern Mediterranean. The sort of thing which constantly came up in fishermen's nets, particularly when they were trawling.

We all went up on deck and got the hatch of the main hold open. Nino and Angelo dropped inside and passed each amphora up in turn. There were four all together and Langley and I manhandled them over the starboard rail.

There was a kind of hiatus afterward and I found myself alone in the prow, smoking a cigarette and looking toward the shore. There was music from the

Bedouin camp beyond the olive grove, some sort of pipes and a drum, insistent, throbbing through the darkness.

Simone said, "There's always something new out of Africa, isn't that what the man said?"

"Something like that," I could smell woodsmoke on the air and it had stopped raining. I said, "What about a drink to celebrate?"

"Celebrate what?"

"The fact that you didn't tell Langley about the Stechkin."

She went very still. "What happened about the Uzi?"

"Now minus a vital portion of its firing pin."

"So you believe I'm on your side?"

I didn't answer, mainly because I didn't want to. For the moment there was no one else on deck, so I pulled in the dinghy and dropped over the rail. "Are you coming?"

I looked up at the face, pale in the subdued glow from the deck light. She said nothing, showed no emotion. Simply climbed over the rail and dropped down beside me. I started the motor and took the dinghy in toward the shore.

Izmir was open for business and welcomed us with delight for we were his only customers. He brought us a bottle of *Verdicchio,* nicely chilled by the waters of the cistern at the back of the house and put his wife to work cooking.

Due mainly to Italian influence, good, traditional Libyan cooking is hard to find these days and the tourist trade isn't helping, but she came up with some sort of fish soup that would have been hard to beat anywhere in the world and a superb dish of *couscous.*

It had stopped raining, the stars were out and a small, sad wind blew in from the sea and rattled the slats of the veranda blinds.

Simone said, "Can we go for a walk? Do you mind?"

"Why not?" I said.

I took the bottle of *Verdicchio* and a glass with us, she kicked off her shoes and we walked along the beach and round the point beyond the palm trees. There wasn't a soul about although we could still hear the music from the Bedu encampment.

She moved down to walk in the shallows. I said, "You want to watch it. You could step on a Portuguese Man o'War or something in the dark."

"I feel like living dangerously." She looked up at the stars. "This is a good night to be alive."

I could have told her that the prospect of an early demise always does have that effect, but I didn't want to spoil it for her.

She said, "I haven't felt like this—not this close to you—since those days at the villa at Cape de Gata."

"Subject made love to Miss Delmas on the terrace."

It was about the cruelest thing I could have said under the circumstances and instantly regretted. She took it like a soldier. "All right, Oliver, I deserved that."

"No, you didn't."

I pulled out a pile of brushwood from under the wood. There were stacks of driftwood around on the beach, most of it damp from the rain, but only superficially. Then I put a match to the brushwood, it all burned readily enough, the flames roaring up into the darkness.

I gave her a cigarette and we sat there roasting ourselves. She said, "Could you go back?"

"To Cape de Gata?" I shrugged. "Only for my things. On the whole it pays to keep moving in this life. Never go back to anything is a fair motto."

"Everyone needs somewhere that's their own," she said. "A place to hide. Roots ..."

"... are people not places," I said, "or so it seems to me."

"You're a truly lonely man," she said. "Because you don't need people. I see that now. Take Hannah, for instance. What have you ever given her except money —material things? How much of yourself?"

"She's better off without me," I said. "It's for her own good."

"Who decides that? You? Did you know that girl thinks the sun rises and sets in you?"

"And you?" I said. "What do you think?"

"If you must know, I think I'd like a swim." She stood up, stripped off her jeans and shirt, bra and pants and simply ran down the beach and into the sea without another word. I almost followed her. Perhaps a year or two earlier I would have done just that, but I was getting too old for such romantic nonsense or so I told myself.

I leaned over to light a cigarette from a splinter. As I looked up, she stepped into the light. Water ran from the firm breasts, glistening in the light of the fire and her body was a thing of mystery, shadowed in the secret places, more beautiful than anything I had ever known.

She stood there for what seemed one of the longest moments in my life and then she smiled and dropped to her knees beside me. As I slipped my arms about her, drawing her close, Langley stepped out of the darkness into the firelight. He was wearing bathing trunks and had obviously just swum ashore.

"So sorry, old stick," he said. "I seem to have dropped in at what's known as an inopportune moment."

Simone stiffened in my arms and then, strangely, relaxed. She said, without turning around, "Do you actually enjoy being what you are, Justin, or do you have to work at it?"

"Oh, dear," he said. "Have I embarrassed you?"

She stood up and turned to face him, hands on hips. "How could you?"

It was the first time I'd seen him really hurt and the effect of her simple reply was almost physical. The smile was wiped clean away and for a moment, there was a kind of desolation there.

As she pulled on her pants and bra, he said, "You bitch—you bloody bitch!"

She totally ignored him, buttoned up her shirt and reached for her jeans. I could have reacted physically, I suppose, but somehow it didn't seem appropriate. I slipped her hand in my arm, we walked away. Perhaps he thought I was afraid—perhaps not. It just didn't seem to matter.

Halfway along the beach and well hidden by darkness, Simone stopped me, reached up and kissed me full on the mouth.

"Thanks," she said.

I was genuinely puzzled. "What on earth for?"

She laughed delightfully. "That's what I love most about you, Oliver. All those brains, all that ruthlessness and inside, you're still a little boy back there on your grandfather's farm running through a field of ripest corn."

But by then she had lost me completely, not that it seemed to matter and we continued into the night, walking back toward the boat, arm in arm.

It was just before nine the following morning when the patrol boat turned up from Tripoli. I was on deck checking the diving equipment with Barzini when Nino gave the alarm.

"There's a boat coming in."

I'd just surfaced after making the first dive of the day and had attached a line to one of the amphorae which Barzini and Angelo were busy hauling in. They got it over the rail and onto the deck where it lay streaming water, looking very impressive what with the mollusks and seashells embedded in it.

I was wearing the top half of an orange wetsuit, a face mask and an aqualung. I came up the access ladder we'd hooked over the rail and said to Langley, "You want to make yourself useful, get one of the other aqualungs on quick and look busy."

He did as he was told without any argument. Simone draped a towel round my shoulders and handed me a lighted cigarette. She was wearing a sweater and jeans. I said, "Go below and get into your bikini. Comb your hair down and wear sunglasses. Anything to gild the lily, then get back up here. Nothing like having a woman around the place to make things look right."

She didn't argue either, which was good because we didn't have much time left to get ready. The boat wasn't much. A shabby old fifty-foot diesel launch that had definitely seen better days and looked capable of fifteen knots at the very most and no more. There were half-a-dozen uniformed sailors on deck and one man stood in the stern behind a Russian RPD light machine-gun, mounted on a swivel and loaded with a hundred-round drum. The red, white, and black tricolor of Libya drooped from a pole behind him.

They came alongside, not too expertly, and Nino and Angelo grabbed the lines they threw. A young officer in a neat khaki uniform and peaked navy cap with what seemed a lavish amount of gold braid in evidence, came out of the wheelhouse and approached the rail.

He straightened his jacket and saluted formally, a handsome young man with a rather melancholy face and a clipped moustache. "I am Lieutenant Ibrahim of the coastguard service. And you?"

"*Palmyra* out of Palermo," I said and snapped my finger to Barzini. "Have you got our papers, Aldo?"

He produced them from the wheelhouse with a great show of joviality and I passed them to Ibrahim. "There you go, lieutenant. Ship's papers and our permit from your own Ministry of the Interior to dive here."

He examined them quickly, a slight frown on his face. "Archaeological diving."

"Yes," I said. "Perhaps you'd care to give us your opinion on this. We've only just brought it up."

His eyes widened when he saw the amphora. "But this is wonderful. What is it—Roman?"

I shook my head. "No, strangely enough it's a Roman wreck we're looking for, but this is Phoenician. Quite unmistakable."

He examined it with awe. "You've found a wreck then?"

"Timber and planking," I said, "And a sternpost. That's all and several more amphorae. I was just going down for another."

Simone appeared from the companionway looking absolutely devastating in a black bikini, gold sandals, dark glasses, and with her hair combed down as I'd suggested. She was carrying a tray containing a bottle of Scotch and several glasses.

Ibrahim, obviously as impressionable as any normal young man, was knocked sideways. I introduced them and he kissed her hand gallantly.

"If you'll excuse me," I said, "I'd like to see what the situation is below."

I nodded to Langley, pulled on my face mask and went over the side. I paused just beneath the surface to adjust my air supply, gave Langley the thumbs up and followed the line down through the smoky green water.

Fifty or sixty feet and I hovered over a great bank of weeds. I could see one amphora just beneath me, another lying on its side in a patch of open sand. Langley appeared beside me, the line in his hand. I signalled to him, he went down and I followed to float over the amphora. We got the line fastened securely, gave the prearranged signal of three tugs and followed it up.

When we broke surface, it was already being hauled over the rail by Nino and Angelo. Ibrahim was standing beside Simone, the glass in his right hand containing enough whiskey to make Mohammed himself spin in his grave.

I went up the ladder behind Langley and unbuckled my aqualung. Ibrahim said, "This is really tremendous."

I said, "Would you like to take one with you, lieutenant? I'm sure the museum authorities in Tripoli would be more than interested. Naturally we'll be in touch with them ourselves before very long to give them a progress report."

"What a wonderful idea," he said, and then the thing misfired slightly. "However, I'll be staying on this section of the coast for the next two days before returning to Tripoli. Perhaps I could pick up the amphora on my way back?"

"But of course," I said.

He turned and kissed Simone's hand again. "Signorina—a delight to be repeated in the not too distant future, I assure you. Gentlemen."

He went back over the rail, Nino and Angelo cast off and the launch moved away. No one spoke until it had negotiated the passage between the Sisters and turned out to sea.

Barzini moved to my shoulder. "What do you think?"

"It worked like a charm," I said. "That's what I think, so now we can get down to more important matters."

I turned, toweling my head and on shore, Zingari's old Ford truck drew up in front of the store.

CHAPTER NINE

CAPE OF FEAR

THE GREEN AND FERTILE LANDSCAPE OF Libya which stretches between the desert and the sea is not unlike southern Italy with olive groves, plantations, vineyards and fields of flowers, but not the Cape Fear section of the coast. There, there was nothing—a place God must have surely forgotten. A hell hole of desert and salt flats and furnace heat.

Langley and Angelo were in the back of the truck and I sat beside Zingari who was obviously as worried as ever. He had provided each of us with a striped cotton burnous of the type worn by many Arabs locally and had begged me to keep the hood up.

We followed the dirt road for several miles, paralleling the single line railway track which, according to Zingari, was only used by the military. Finally, it left the road, looping away into a wilderness of jagged ridges and defiles no more than a mile or two from the sea.

After a while, Zingari pulled off the road and drove up into a narrow, rocky valley. He switched off the engine. "Now we walk," he said and got out.

We followed him to the end of the valley and along a defile with a few thorn bushes on its rim and he whispered, "Very quiet now and great care. We are close to the prison. Very close."

I eased up under a thorn bush with my binoculars and found myself looking down at the main gates of the prison which were no more than a hundred yards away.

A file of wretched looking convicts in leg irons shuffled past on the far side of the road under armed guard, each man carrying a pick or a shovel. There was a sudden shrill whistle from not too far away and a railway engine came round the bend pulling several boxcars.

It had been a long time since I'd seen a steam engine and I examined it closely. It pulled up in front of the main prison gates which opened and a file of soldiers moved out to meet it. At the same time, the passengers on the train got out and waited beside it. There were a few convicts in chains, but the majority were soldiers.

Everyone was searched meticulously and at the same time another squad searched the train. Finally the passengers passed through the main gates on foot and the train followed, passing through into the compound. The gates were closed and all was still again.

"What about the women?" I asked Zingari.

He pointed to a judas in the main gate. "They pass through there in single file. I'll have forty-three tonight."

"Forty-four with the sweetheart of the forces, here," Langley said.

Angelo glanced sharply at him, real dislike in his eyes. "Why don't you try buttoning your lip for a change?"

"Oh, dear, have I upset him?"

You didn't have to be a genius to see in which area the basic tension lay between them, but in any event, I intervened quickly.

"Cut it out, you two, and that's an order." Angelo turned and went back to the truck angrily. I said to Langley, "Any more cracks like that out of you and you walk back. Understand?"

"Didn't mean any harm, old stick. Only a joke," he said, but there was more to it than that. It showed in his eyes.

We got back in the truck and drove back along the road past the turn-off to Gela. Zabia was another seven or eight miles further on. A sprawling sort of place with a population of three thousand. White houses dotted among the palm trees, a market in the main square.

Zingari's bar was on the waterfront of the small harbor. *Cafe Zingari,* the sign said above the door and certainly the tables under the awning at the front were crowded enough. He took the truck round to a walled courtyard at the rear and we were admitted by a private door.

Someone was playing a very bad piano and there was laughter faintly in the distance. The room he took us into was obviously his own and furnished handsomely enough as a cross between an office and a living room. There was a desk and two or three chairs, a daybed, Persian rugs on the floor.

There was a bottle of whiskey and several glasses standing on a Damascus tray on his desk as if by prior arrangement. He poured everybody a drink and took one himself.

"Finest Scotch, Mr. Grant. You see the label on the bottle?"

I didn't say anything and he smiled nervously and drank a little whiskey. "Right, now I show you a few of the women."

He opened a shutter in the far wall and I moved to join him. Through the slots of the blind on the other side I could see down into a bar that was literally full of whores of just about every size, shape and description. If they had one thing in common it was probably the fact that they'd all very definitely seen better days.

Langley said, "My God, you'll look like the Queen of the May when you get in among that little lot, Carter. Every soldier in the fort will be sniffing around as if you were a bitch in heat."

Angelo punched him in the face and Langley was good, I had to give him that, turning instantly so that the knuckles only grazed his cheek.

He pivoted on one hip and threw Angelo across the desk. Something went with a distinct crack, but Angelo came up on his feet and caught Langley with a good solid punch under the ribs that drove the breath from his body.

Langley grunted and swayed there, apparently defenseless and Angelo fell for it. He swung wildly, forgetting everything he'd ever been taught, and Langley grabbed for the right arm, pushed it round and up in a vicelike grip, running Angelo's face into the wall. Angelo went down and didn't get up again.

The whole affair from beginning to end had lasted no longer than five or six seconds. Too quick for me to interfere, but now I pushed Langley violently to one side and dropped to one knee beside Angelo.

He was groaning slightly, shaking his head, which didn't surprise me in the slightest as his nose was obviously very badly broken and there was a great deal of blood in evidence. Zingari passed me a jug of water and a napkin. I soaked it quickly and wiped away the blood. He opened his eyes almost instantly and looked up at me with a complete lack of comprehension. Something clicked and he tried to sit up. He cried out in pain and clutched at his left side. It was obvious at once that he had one or more ribs fractured.

I turned on Langley. "You stupid bastard. Do you realize what you've done?"

He wasn't smiling now, and when he laughed it was forced and hearty. "Come on, old stick. Nothing to write home about there. He's playing you up."

There were beads of sweat on Angelo's face and his mouth was clenched in agony. "Is there a doctor in Zabia?" I asked Zingari.

He nodded. "I'll send someone for him."

Langley sat in the corner looking sullen. I had another whiskey and waited. The doctor came quite quickly, a small balding man in a neat brown gabardine suit. He gave Angelo an injection, diagnosed two broken ribs and strapped them up. There was nothing he could do about the nose. That needed an expert surgeon. He departed after obtaining his fee in cash from Zingari, leaving a bottle of painkilling tablets.

I could have shot Langley out of hand, but that would hardly have improved the situation. Zingari was beside himself with anxiety. "But what will we do, signor? Everything is ready." And then, as a sudden wild hope struck him, "Maybe you won't be able to go through with it now? Yes, that's it. We'll have to abandon the whole crazy scheme."

"We'll return to Gela," I said. "We'll decide what to do then. Now give me a hand."

He did as he was told with obvious reluctance, helping me take Angelo out to the truck. Langley, for once, was silent, stunned I think, by the enormity of what had happened. We put Angelo up in the cab, I sat beside him and Langley rode in the rear on his own.

Angelo did very well considering, although it was obvious that the painkilling injection had helped considerably. "Don't worry about me," he said. "It's nothing. I'm going to be fine."

I don't know who he was trying to kid the most. Himself or me, but by the time we reached Gela and pulled up at the pier, it had become obvious that he wasn't being particularly successful in either direction.

I left him in his bunk in the forward cabin with Simone seeing to him and went into the saloon. Barzini sat at the head of the table, the whiskey bottle in one hand, a glass in the other, looking like thunder.

"Now what happens?" he demanded.

I shrugged. "I don't know. He says he'll be able to get by if he swallows enough pain-killers beforehand, but I don't think it's likely. And then there's his face. It's bad enough now. By this evening it'll be so swollen he'll be unrecognizable."

Barzini turned on Langley who sat on one of the bench seats looking defiant. "You bastard, are you satisfied now you've ruined everything? What do we do? Without someone on the inside to pull up that climbing rope we've had it."

"Then you really don't have any choice, do you?" Simone said from the cabin door. "You'll have to send me."

I said, "Don't be a bloody fool!" more as a reflex action than anything else.

It was noticeable that Barzini made no comment. He sat looking at her gravely and beyond him Langley was frowning.

"Let's get it straight," Barzini said. "You'd have to go in with the other girls, handle whoever grabs you on the way in, drop him as soon as you can and make your way up to the north wall."

"Where she'll have to dispose of two sentries," I said. "Be your age, Aldo, the whole thing is crazy. She wouldn't stand a chance."

"Who knows?" he said. "With a gun in the hand all things are possible, and I'll have to go in with you now, of course. You're going to need another man."

"It's worth a try, isn't it, Oliver?" she said. "I mean, we can't just turn back after having come all this way."

I took her by the shoulders, "It's just not on. God knows what could happen to you on the way in, and then the two sentries." I shook my head. "It's impossible."

And yet I think I knew inside me that I was talking for the sake of talking. As she'd said herself, she was our only chance. There was no one else.

She said quietly, "What are you speaking with, Oliver, your head or your heart?"

To which there could really be only one reply, so I turned to Zingari. "All right, everything goes according to the original plan except you take her instead of Carter."

He looked completely crushed, mainly at finding the whole thing was still on, I suppose. "All right, signor, if you insist. The girls will be delivered in two trucks at nine o'clock. I'll be drivinßg the second one myself. I'll stop here outside the store at eight-thirty to pick her up."

Simone said, "I'll be ready."

Zingari shook his head. "Crazy. The whole stinking world is getting crazier day by day. Can I go now, signor?"

I ran him across to the pier in the dinghy and took my time coming back. The more I thought about it the less I liked it, but the truth of it now was quite simply that there was no other choice.

We spent the rest of the afternoon getting the equipment ready. The uniforms were no problem as Barzini had included half a dozen in the first place to cover all eventualities. The Libyan Army at that time, like most paramilitary organizations throughout the world, favored camouflaged battledresses and Africa Korps caps. All very sinister-looking.

We had a Russian AK assault rifle each plus a hundred and eighty additional rounds in belt bandoliers and I had a Stechkin machine pistol. On top of that there were three Sturma stick grenades per man, not to mention a couple of two hundred foot coils of finest hemp climbing rope, Nino having refused nylon with contempt.

Simone, of course, was going to have to wear Angelo's clothes. She took them off with her to the aft cabin to get ready. She was to wear a loose-fitting mini dress with a smock front and before she put it on I went in and helped her wind two hundred feet of twine around her waist. She also had a rubber electric torch to fasten to the end of the twine and lower from the ramparts to give us some guidance as we waited on the cliffs below.

She took the whole thing with astonishing calm, including the moment when Barzini appeared with a Ceska automatic, fully loaded with a four-inch silencer on the end, which he put in her handbag. He also produced a switchblade knife and a roll of surgical tape.

"I'll tape the knife to your right thigh," he said. "Don't forget it's there."

She pressed the button with her thumb. The razor-sharp blade sprang into view and she shuddered. "I could never use a thing like that on anyone."

"You'll just have to wait and see like the rest of us, won't you?" Barzini told her roughly. He taped the knife in position and went out.

Simone pulled the dress over her head and adjusted it, then she combed her hair. She really did look very pretty. I said, "You look too good. If Masmoudi sees you, he'll grab you himself."

"We'll see," she said, and for the first time that night, smiled. "You'd better take me ashore now."

The others were silent when we went through the saloon, but as I handed her into the dinghy, Langley came out on deck. He leaned over the rail and said awkwardly, "Look, I'm sorry about the way things have worked out—okay?"

She said, "Is that supposed to make it all right?"

"Oh, go to hell," he said and turned away as I pressed the starter and took the dinghy in toward the shore.

We waited in the shadows by the store, not that we had long for I could hear the truck coming for quite some time, the engine clear on the night air.

"Well, this is it," I said as it reached the olive grove.

She cracked then, for a moment only, flinging herself into my arms, kissing me. And then she pulled away.

"If you die on me, I'll never forgive you," I said.

It was a poor attempt at humor. She blew me a kiss, a strangely personal act that touched me deeply, smiled and turned and walked toward the truck as it pulled up.

There was a great deal of shouting and singing coming from inside. In fact, a good many of the girls sounded fairly drunk to me. Perhaps they needed to be. Not a pleasant thought. She climbed up in the cab beside Zingari and he drove away. I stood there in the shadows, listening to the sound of the engine dwindling and after a while there was nothing. So that was very much that and I turned and went back to the dinghy.

When I reached *Palmyra,* Barzini, Nino, and Langley were waiting on deck, all in battledress. I left them to load the equipment and went below and changed myself. Strange to be in uniform again. It had been a hell of a long time. Once I had enjoyed this kind of thing.

As I went up the companionway I was conscious of neither optimism nor despair. As a matter of interest, the only thing I could think about was Simone and that would never do. It was not, after all, my style, as she would have been the first to remind me.

The others were ready and waiting in the inflatable dinghy, the outboard motor ticking over. I dropped in beside them. Angelo, who had hauled himself up from the cabin to see us off, waved from the rail.

And then we were away, moving out to sea between the Sisters and the game was finally afoot.

There was supposed to be a full moon, which had worried me in the planning stage, but the weather was on our side and it wasn't much in evidence. Low cloud, light sea mist and a fine drifting rain kept visibility down to a minimum.

We stayed about half a mile off shore, too close in to run into any tunny boats and yet because of the poor visibility, well out of sight of shore. Which meant, of course, that I had to rely on dead reckoning, making the final run-in blind.

At the last possible moment, I killed the motor and we took to the oars. Not the best of solutions, considering the conditions, but taking the noise factor into account we didn't really have any other choice.

For a few rather nasty minutes I thought we'd made a bad mistake. The dinghy, minus the power of the outboard motor, heeled, water pouring over the gunnel for a stiff offshore breeze was lifting the waves into whitecaps.

Barzini and Langley had a pair of oars each and rowed like hell which they needed to do for there was a four or five knot current running as I'd expected from the chart.

The shore was plain to see now, mainly because of the surf, white in the darkness as it pounded across the beach. And once, for a moment only, the moon showed through a rent in the clouds and I could see the fortress waiting for us up there on the cliffs.

We were moving in very fast now, caught in a current of such strength that there was nothing we could do except to try to keep floating and hang on. The sea filled the darkness with its roaring, shaking and tearing at the beach with great angry sucking noises.

We bounced off a rock, spinning round in a circle and Langley lost an oar. For a moment or so, we were quite helpless, dirty white foam boiling around us and I saw, in my mind's eye, the whole thing finished before it got started.

Nino cried out a warning and I glanced over my shoulder as a long comber rolled out of the darkness, a six footer with a white, curling head on it. I thought it was the final end of things. Instead, it was our salvation for it carried us straight in over the rocks to a great bank of shingle.

I was over the side in a moment and so were the others, pushing and hauling at the dinghy to get her up to dry land. Another wave flooded in, boiling around our knees as if determined to have us back. It retreated fast and a moment later, we were over the top of the shingle bank and moving up the beach.

We deposited the dinghy in soft white sand at the very base of the cliffs and Langley said, "Christ Almighty, I'm soaked to the bloody skin."

"We're here, aren't we?" Barzini said. "That's all that matters."

He produced a thermos of hot coffee from one of the rucksacks in the dinghy and passed it round. I looked up through the rain and darkness to the ramparts. There were a couple of lights up there, but otherwise no sign of life.

Langley said, "She was delivered at nine. It's now ten o'clock. That means she's had an hour up there. Where is she?"

"Give her time," I said. "She'll be there."

He shook his head. "You're kidding yourself, Grant. She isn't going to make it. There was never any chance that she would in the first place."

"Why don't you shut up?" Barzini told him. "She's got more in her than you have, that girl, Langley. I think maybe she's going to surprise you."

Langley turned away angrily. I sat down under an overhang of rock to get some shelter from the rain and lit a cigarette. I was damned cold and very wet, but I wasn't worried or at least that's what I told myself, and whenever I thought of what might be happening to her up there, I pushed that thought away.

So we waited and the rain drifted in and the surf pounded the beach and nothing happened—not a damned thing. And then it was midnight and the plain ugly fact of the matter could no longer be avoided.

In the end it was Barzini who came over and squatted beside me. "Not so good, Oliver," he said.

I nodded wearily. "Not so good, Aldo."

CHAPTER TEN

SIMONE ALONE

INSIDE THE CAB OF THE OLD truck it was hot and uncomfortable and stank of diesel fumes. Zingari was an indifferent driver and they bounced along over the dirt road to a chorus of protest from the women in the rear. Someone banged on the partition and made a suggestion in Italian, using language as foul as it was possible to imagine.

He turned to Simone, his pale, rat-like face shining with sweat in the subdued light of the dashboard. "They are a bad lot back there. Straight from the gutter."

"They seem to serve your purpose," she said.

He shrugged. "The world is as it is, signorina. I didn't make the rules."

She struggled to contain her anger, aware of the contempt she felt for this foul little man. "I wonder how it would be if they decided to turn?" she said. "Got their hands on you."

He glanced at her, startled, the face yellow with fear, and forced a smile. "Hardly likely, signorina. They have nowhere to go. This is—how do the Americans say it?—the end of the line."

For me, too? she wondered. The thought chilled her clear to the bone and instinctively, she put a hand on the top of her thigh, feeling the knife that Barzini had taped into position there. How could she use it? How could she possibly use such a weapon?

She became aware that Zingari was glancing sideways at her and when she looked down saw that the skirt of the mini dress was stretched taut, exposing the nylon thighs. She tried to pull it down, but found it impossible.

Zingari's tongue flickered across his lips; he was sweating harder than ever, the smell sour and offensive in that confined space. She challenged him with her gaze and he tried another of those weak smiles.

"You are too beautiful, signorina. Compared to the pigs in the rear, you will shine out like a torch in the darkness."

"And what do you suggest I do about it?"

"There's an old burnous behind your seat. Try that."

She pulled it out and unfolded it across her knees. It was typical of the kind of thing worn by Arabs of both sexes. An ankle-length mantle with a pointed hood in blue and white stripes.

Zingari slipped a hand under the mantle and squeezed her thigh. He smiled ingratiatingly. "Cover up those lovely legs, eh, signorina? Keep you out of trouble?"

Her handbag was on the floor beside her left ankle. She reached down, took out the Ceska and held it in her lap, the ugly, bulbous silencer pointing straight at him. "Touch me again," she said calmly. "Just once more ..."

He withdrew his hand hurriedly, the truck swerved from one side of the road to the other. There was another chorus of screams from inside.

"Signorina, please. I would not offend you for the world."

He was shaking like a leaf and the smell of his sweat seemed to sharpen, grow even more pungent. She leaned into the corner, her face to the window, holding the Ceska concealed in a fold of the burnous. The fine rain blowing in off the sea carried salt with it and she thought of Grant and no one else. Wondered where he was now and what was happening to him.

The moon appeared through the clouds and for an instant she saw the sea and beyond it, at the end of a great spur of rock, the fortress of Râs Kanai. *Cape of Fear.* It was well named. As it disappeared from view, she hugged herself tightly, suddenly terrified.

The women in the first truck were already getting out as they arrived. The floodlighting over the main gate was turned on illuminating the whole scene. A small gate to one side stood open and two or three soldiers in camouflaged uniforms stood outside. An enormous black-bearded man with sergeant's stripes on his sleeve stood a yard or two in front of them, hands on hips, a cigarette in his mouth, looking the women over.

"That's Husseini, the senior n.c.o.," Zingari said to Simone. "Don't fall into his hands, signorina. You'll never be the same again. Now put the burnous on and wait on the other side of the truck."

He got out and went round to the rear. Simone heard him shouting at the women, the chorus of catcalls he received in reply. She slipped out of the cab, pulled the burnous over her head and waited in the shadows.

The women from the second truck started to move forward to join the others. Zingari went round to the other side of the cab and reached inside to switch off the lights.

"Signorina?" he called softly. "Get in among the women. Lose yourself in the crowd and pray. There is nothing more I can do for you."

She felt calm then for no reason that made any kind of sense. Ice-cool as she pulled the hood of her burnous about her face, she moved round the tail of the truck and joined the other women.

They were as foul as she had imagined. Many of them partly drunk, some completely. Most of them were old or looked old, ravaged by years of squalor and disease. There were very few Arabs as was to be expected, but a considerable number of Italians, the sweepings, from the sound of their accent, of the slums of Naples.

Simone pressed on into the center of that jostling throng. No one took the slightest notice of her, most of them being totally occupied in calling to soldiers up on the wall above the gate. A large, fat woman in front of Simone with hair so red that it could only have come out of a bottle, stumbled drunkenly as she crossed the raised railway line outside the gate and fell flat on her face. She tried to get up and failed and the others flooded past, several of them trampling on her.

It was a heaven-sent opportunity. Simone got her to her feet, not without considerable difficulty, an arm around her shoulders and moved on with the crowd, the woman moaning drunkenly.

The onward rush slowed down for a while as the women passed in through the narrow gate, two or three at a time. Sergeant Husseini stood watching, the great bearded face expressionless and yet Simone felt that there was nothing that escaped him. That he saw everything there was to see. The eyes seemed to fasten on hers, she turned her face down and moved on, clutching the other woman tightly. A moment later and they were through the narrow gate and moving along a dark tunnel, finally emerging into an enormous courtyard.

The women milled around in an unruly mob, but staying together. Beyond them were the soldiers, a gap of thirty or forty yards between the two groups. The women jeered and catcalled, shouting obscenities and the men replied in kind.

Simone looked around the square quickly, taking everything in. The ramparts, the great iron-barred gate to the main building which presumably housed the prisoners. The railway train Grant had mentioned stood on the far side, beside the main building. There were half a dozen boxcars, two or three flat-tops, as far as she could see, but the locomotive itself was standing inside what was obviously an engine shed.

Most surprising of all, in the far corner of the compound a pleasant villa in the Italian colonial style stood in a lush garden surrounded by a low wall.

To the right of her were several small buildings, presumably storehouses, and several trucks were parked, all in an area of deep shadow. She eased her arm away from the woman beside her, leaning her against the wall and started to edge away through the crowd toward the concealing darkness and, suddenly, everyone went silent.

It was really quite remarkable. As if someone had turned off a switch. An iron gate in the wall surrounding the house had opened and a man was walking across the courtyard.

Like the other soldiers present he wore a camouflaged uniform. The only difference was that he was bareheaded and wore no badges of rank and yet Simone knew there was only one person this could be.

Colonel Masmoudi paused in the center of the courtyard between the two groups. He had a swagger stick in one hand which he tapped restlessly against his right thigh. Sergeant Husseini moved in smartly and saluted. Colonel Masmoudi raised the swagger stick briefly. He was a handsome man with a heavy dark moustache. There was a brief exchange in Arabic. Simone couldn't understand a word, but the contempt on Masmoudi's face was enough.

His eyes traveled over the women casually. He started to turn away and at that precise moment, the fat woman leaning against the wall seemed to regain her senses. She cried out incoherently and lurched forward, grabbing at Simone and pulling down the hood of her burnous.

Masmoudi turned. Simone seemed to feel his eyes burn into hers. He stood there staring at her in the silence, then said something to Sergeant Husseini, who walked into the crowd very quietly, scattering the women roughly on either side of him.

The fat woman pawed at him, smiling archly. He pushed her violently away, grabbed Simone by the arm, and propelled her in front of him through the crowd. She fought to control the panic that surged inside her, for fear would not help her now, and schooled herself to play her part.

She kept her head down, Masmoudi tapped her under the chin with his swagger stick and she looked into the dark eyes. "What are you, Italian?" he asked in that language.

She shook her head and said in a low voice, "No, colonel, I'm from Marseilles."

"Ah, a Frenchwoman." He switched to excellent French without any apparent difficulty. "How the hell do you come to be here with this heap of filth?"

"An old friend invited me to stay with him in Tripoli for a while. When I arrived, he'd moved on." She shrugged. "I'd very little money. It didn't last long."

"And then you met Zingari."

She managed to sound angry. "The swine didn't tell me it would be like this."

"Never mind. It may well prove a most fortunate occurrence for both of us." He took her arm and said casually over his shoulder, "All yours, sergeant."

Husseini gave them enough time to get clear then shouted something unintelligible that was drowned in the immediate uproar as the two groups rushed together. Simone glanced over her shoulder. It was an incredible sight, a scene from hell with the damned pulling and tearing at each other in a shouting, struggling, heaving mass of bodies in the light from the floodlamps.

"Don't look back," Masmoudi told her. "That's feeding time at the zoo. Something to keep the animals happy. Not for you."

"Don't you believe in the equality of men then?" she said. "I understood you were a Communist."

He opened the garden gate and pushed her inside. "A magnificent absurdity. God made some men big, some small among other things."

"God?" she said. "Does he still enter into your scheme of things?"

They had reached the steps leading up to the veranda of the house and he paused, turning to look at her, a slightly quizzical frown on his face. "I think there is more to you than meets the eye, little flower," he said.

Her mouth went dry. This was not the man she had expected. Handsome, shrewd, even gentle if he wanted to be, she was sure of that. He in no way filled Zingari's description.

She said desperately, trying to be coy, "Hidden depths."

"Who knows?" He smiled faintly, opened the front door and led her inside.

It was comfortably furnished, but no more than that. A soldier's room. Table, chairs, a large divan piled high with cushions, shelves filled with books.

As he closed the door, he took her handbag from her and dropped it on a chair. There wasn't a thing she could do about that and he slipped his arms about her waist from the rear, pulling her close against him.

Quite suddenly he flung her forward across the cushions of the divan, holding her down with one hand and considerable strength. He pulled up the burnous, slipped a hand under the hem of her skirt and felt for the springblade knife.

"What have we got here?"

He pulled it away roughly, the surgical tape tearing free so that she cried out in pain. He held up the knife and sprang the blade. He laughed then, his mouth wide.

"Oh, a young lady of considerable depth, I can see that." He flipped the knife across the room to bury itself in a cupboard door.

"I didn't know what to expect," Simone said. "I only wanted to protect myself."

As he released her, she turned, the burnous opened and the hem of the cotton mini dress slipped back, exposing the thighs. Masmoudi's eyes sparkled fire; he ran a hand up each clad leg from ankle to thigh and smiled.

"You know something, little flower? I'm going to enjoy you." She felt her stomach grow weak, some deep, instinctual response moving inside her as he stood over her, hands on hips. "Yes, definitely an occasion. In fact, a champagne occasion. Wait there. I'll be right back."

He crossed the room, opened a louvred door and disappeared. Simone was on her feet in an instant and went after him. She peered through the slats of the door into a kitchen. Masmoudi opened the door of a large icebox and took out a bottle of champagne. She turned away at once, tiptoed across the room, picked up her handbag and let herself out.

She hurried down the path to the garden gate. It was all quiet now, the soldiers presumably having taken the women to their quarters, but the floodlighting was still on making it impossible to cross the square directly.

She worked her way round, keeping to the shadows, pulling the hood of the burnous close about her face and had barely reached the far side and the shelter of the vehicles parked in the shadows when Masmoudi's front door was flung open and he appeared on the veranda.

"Husseini!" he called at the top of his voice.

Simone darted up a flight of stone steps to a higher level, keeping to the wall. Up there she was in total darkness and when she looked down she saw Sergeant Husseini quite clearly doubling across the square. He was stripped to the waist and had no boots on.

She started to feel her way up another flight of stone steps cautiously and the sounds of activity in the courtyard below increased so that by the time she had reached the next level there were at least two dozen soldiers down there in the courtyard. And then, to her dismay, a voice called out in Arabic somewhere high above her, a torch was switched on and someone started to come down.

She descended the steps as quickly as the darkness allowed, pausing only when she reached the lower level, for to go down into the courtyard was to invite certain capture.

There was an iron rail. She leaned against it, looking about her desperately, aware of the sound of boots descending the steps above her and then she noticed the roof of one of the trucks four or five feet below, projecting from inside some sort of shed.

It was her only hope and as the steps grew nearer, she slipped under the rail, dropped onto the canvas roof, crawled inside the overhang and lay down. She looked at her watch. It was almost ten o'clock. She took the Ceska from her handbag, held it in her left hand, finger on the trigger, and waited, face against the canvas, while they beat the yard for her below.

It was eleven o'clock before they gave up, half-past before she could be sure. She lay there waiting, listening to the silence, trying to satisfy herself as to its totality before finally crawling back outside, reaching up for the railings and pulling herself up onto the landing. She barely hesitated before starting up the next flight of steps.

Time was of the essence now and it occurred to her that Grant and the others, ready and waiting for at least two hours on the beach, could only be imagining the worst.

It started to rain quite heavily as she went up the last few steps to the ramparts of the north wall. She hesitated, keeping to the shadows for a moment. There was a lamp of some sort twenty or thirty yards further on. A soldier stood beside it sheltering in the corner where two walls joined.

There was no sign of the other sentry which was unfortunate, but further delay was impossible so she stepped out of the shadows. As she walked, she unfastened the front of the burnous so that it fell open.

At the sound of her approach, the sentry came to life and moved into the open, his AK assault rifle at the ready. He lowered it just as quickly, his mouth gaping, for now she had moved into the area of light and made a reasonably spectacular figure in the flowing, hooded mantle and brief mini skirt.

He spoke to her in Arabic and she answered in Italian, "Hello, darling, got a cigarette?"

He hesitated then produced a packet from his tunic pocket and said, "What are you doing up here?"

"Oh, I was with one of the sergeants. He was drunk and I got bored so I thought I'd look for a little fresh air."

She leaned back against the wall, raising one knee slightly, arching her body provocatively. He moved a little closer, a glazed look in his eyes and put a hand on her right thigh. At the same moment the other sentry appeared from the darkness a few yards away.

He called out in Arabic. Simone leaned forward, cupped her hand very deliberately between the first sentry's legs, and breathed in his ear. "Can't you send him away for a while?"

The sentry didn't even hesitate. He propped his AK in an angle in the wall, turned, and advanced on his comrade. There was a rapid conversation in low tones, a certain amount of arm-waving, and the second sentry turned and disappeared into the darkness.

He turned and came toward her. "We're entitled to coffee at this time of night," he said. "He's gone to get it. I've told him to take his time."

"That's good," she said, producing the Ceska from her handbag and cocking it. "Now, do exactly as you're told and you'll be all right."

He stood very still for a long, long moment, staring at her and then he threw back his head and laughed and came forward.

"No," she said, panic moving inside her. "Please!" And she was holding the Ceska in both hands.

He looked angry now, teeth bared wolfishly, and reached out to grab, leaving her very little choice. She pulled the trigger, the silenced Ceska coughed once in the heavy rain. A hole appeared an inch above the right eye, he staggered back over the platform edge and disappeared into darkness.

It was like a dream barely remembered on waking and already fading as she turned, swallowing the bile that rose in her throat. She picked up her handbag and hurried back along the ramparts out of the circle of light, stopping where a half turret, which had once obviously housed a gun, projected into space.

She pulled up her dress and unwound the two-hundred-foot line of thin twine as fast as she could, turning herself again and again until she was dizzy. It took far longer than she had imagined and by the time it was finally free she was sweating heavily and quite exhausted. When she took the torch from her handbag and threaded the end of the twine through the wire loop, her fingers trembled.

She paused, listening hard, but there was still no sign of the other sentry returning and she leaned out of one of the embrasures in the turret, switched on the torch, and started to lower it.

There wasn't much left in hand when there was a sudden sharp tug that almost had it through her fingers although as she'd looped the end round her waist she couldn't have lost it altogether. She waited. After a while there was another sharp tug and she started to haul in the line.

In a surprisingly short space of time the end of the main climbing rope appeared. Nino had spliced the end into a large loop which she dropped over one of the stone columns between two of the embrasures.

There was a long pause. She waited, shaking like a leaf, suddenly ice-cold in the driving rain, reaction, she supposed.

A cheerful voice said, "Heh, angel, you're a sight for sore eyes," and Nino hauled himself in through the embrasure.

She hugged him eagerly. "Is everything all right?"

"Sure." He busied himself unloading the large rucksack he'd carried on his back as well as his rifle. "You had us worried."

He had the second coil of climbing rope in his hand already and was paying it out into the darkness. "What happens now?" she said.

"They climb the main rope and I help them on the way with this."

"Will it be all right?"

He grinned, his teeth white in the darkness. "What the English climbers in the Alps call a piece of cake."

She pulled the burnous closer about her, shivering in that driving rain, watching as Nino brought the rope in slowly and steadily over his left shoulder and under the right arm. He only stopped once and then for no more than a second or two and then, quite suddenly, another dim figure appeared in the embrasure.

She moved forward uncertainly. "Are you all right?"

"Simone?" A familiar voice said, and Grant reached out through the darkness, pulling her close, holding her to him. It was only then that she stopped shaking.

CHAPTER ELEVEN

TO THE DARK TOWER

IT WAS BARZINI WHO FIRST SAW the lighted torch bobbing down on the end of the line no more than forty or fifty feet to the right of us. I don't think I've ever experienced a feeling of such profound relief. She was all right—that was my first and most immediate thought.

We gathered up the equipment between us and moved into position. Nino himself uncoiled the climbing rope and attached it to the line. He gave a tug, the agreed signal, and it was immediately drawn up.

"What in the hell took her so long?" Langley whispered.

Not that he could have expected an answer. I said, "Does it matter? She made it, didn't she?"

Nino was busy getting his rucksack on. He slung his rifle over his back and tested the rope. He grinned and put a hand on my shoulder. "Okay, here we go. Pray for me."

From the sound of it the young devil was enjoying himself. A stone rattled under his boot and a moment later he had disappeared upward into the darkness.

I had expected a lengthy wait and was caught unaware when the second rope snaked down over the rocks and fell across my shoulders. I was next in line, Langley to follow, with Barzini bringing up the rear. I tied the rope securely about my waist with a running bowline and gave a tug. The slack was immediately taken up and I reached for the main climbing rope.

"Good luck," Barzini whispered and I started to climb.

It was something of an anticlimax. For one thing, as Nino had said, it was better in the darkness because if you looked down there was nothing to see anyway so there was not even an illusion of height and the cliff was much easier than Zingari had suggested—a gradual incline with a broken surface of granite and basalt that gave good footholds in spite of the rain. And the safety line was of tremendous assistance, Nino pulling on it so strongly that most of the time it felt as if I was being hauled up, no strain on the arms at all.

I paused only once as I went over the edge of the cliff itself and found myself on a ledge beneath the wall. He started to pull again and it was only then in scaling the final thirty feet or so that I felt any strain on the arms at all.

A few moments later I scrambled in through the embrasure and found myself on firm ground inside the turret.

There were two figures, dimly seen. Simone said, "Are you all right?"

I reached forward and pulled her into my arms.

Langley was with us in a matter of minutes. Barzini was more of a problem and in the end had the three of us on the rope hauling him by brute force. We dragged him in through the embrasure and he fell on his hands and knees, panting for breath.

"Mother of God," he whispered. "Never again—never in this world."

I helped him to his feet and as he untied himself Nino said urgently, "Someone's coming."

"The other sentry," Simone said.

"What did you do with the first?" Langley asked her.

"I had to shoot him."

"Did you, by God." There was something close to admiration in Langley's voice. He said, "I'll handle this, old stick," and slipped off.

The sentry stood under the lamp a few yards away calling softly in Arabic. He started toward us uncertainly and Langley moved out of the darkness behind him and put a hand over the man's throat. A knife blade gleamed dully in the yellow light, the sentry grunted, and Langley dragged him back into the shadows.

He was whistling softly between his teeth when he rejoined us. "All light, old stick," he said cheerfully. "What's next?"

"Masmoudi," I said, and led the way along the ramparts until we could look down into the lighted courtyard below. "That's his house on the other side of the square."

"I've already been there once tonight," Simone said and quickly explained what had happened.

When she was finished, I said, "All right, we'll go in as arranged, looking like some duty detail—Langley up front in case his Arabic is needed, Simone in the center." I put a hand on her arm. "If anyone's around to see it will look as if you're in custody, although from the sound of it, I'd say the garrison's likely to be occupied in other matters tonight."

We went down the series of stone steps that led to the courtyard, moved into the temporary shelter of the parked truck and took up position. Then I simply gave a whispered command and we struck off across the square, Langley leading.

The rain hammered down, bouncing from the cobbles. We didn't see a soul, although the sentry on the wall above the main gate must have seen us unless he was sheltering from the downpour. Just in case, I gave Simone the occasional rough push on the way across to make it look good.

Langley opened the gate and we moved through the garden and up the steps to the veranda. The shutters were closed and Langley leaned down and peered through the slats.

He turned and said with a grin, "He would appear to be occupied."

I looked for myself. Masmoudi was sitting stripped to the waist and drinking a glass of champagne. The woman who lay stretched out on the divan beside him, one knee raised, was down to her underwear.

I nodded to Barzini, who waited, a hand on the door knob. It opened to his touch, he moved in quickly, covering Masmoudi with his assault rifle and the rest of us crowded in after him.

Masmoudi didn't even blink. He sat there, the glass of champagne in his hand, looking us over and then he smiled at Simone. "So there you are, little flower." He spoke to her in French. "I said you had depths."

"Let's stick to Italian," I told him. "That way we'll all stay happy."

The woman on the divan opened her mouth as if to scream and Langley jammed a hand over it. "You mustn't do that," he said. "Very naughty."

She was probably no more than twenty-seven or eight but had definitely seen better days. Simone said, "Was she all you could get?"

Masmoudi sighed. "One has to do the best one can. It's not often that one like you comes our way out here in the wilderness, little flower. I should have known it was too good to be true."

She seemed amused. "You could have looked a little harder."

"Ah, but you see, I thought you'd run off with one of my men. I decided that must be the real reason you'd come in with the usual rabble. I intended to parade every man in the place in the morning and keep them out there on the square until I got to the bottom of the matter."

The woman on the divan groaned. Langley pulled her up by the hair and dragged her across to a closet. "Now be a good girl and shut up," he said cheerfully. "If you don't I'll cut your throat."

He shoved her inside the closet, closed the door then walked back to the table and helped himself to a glass of champagne. "Life really is full of pleasant surprises," he said. "This is good. Very, very good."

"But hardly the reason for such enterprise," Masmoudi said. "To what do I owe this rather dubious pleasure?"

"You have a prisoner here," I told him. "A young American named Wyatt."

He showed no particular reaction. "So?"

"We want him."

"Ah, I see now. And if I comply? What then?"

"We drive out through that gate with you along for insurance. Not far. Just a few miles up the coast."

"And what happens there?"

"We head out to sea, back where we came from, and you can do what you damn well please."

"With a bullet in the head?"

"No percentage in it. What would be the point?"

"It sounds plausible enough when you put it like that." He reached for his shirt. "What happens if I refuse?"

Nino took an ivory Madonna from his pocket. When he pressed the feet, a wicked-looking stiletto jumped into view. "Ingenious," Masmoudi said. "But then the Italians have always been culturally inclined, even in matters of violence."

"First the right ear, then the left," Nino said. "Do we understand each other?"

"Perfectly."

Masmoudi reached for the telephone and Langley said, "I should point out that I speak rather good Arabic, so behave yourself."

"I always do, my friend, especially in situations like this, I assure you."

He spoke briefly into the telephone in Arabic and replaced the receiver. Langley said, "He spoke to the guardroom. Told them to get a Sergeant Husseini to collect convict eight-thirty-three from the special block and bring him here."

I said, "This special block. Is that as bad as it sounds?"

"Your friend Wyatt has been a little difficult," Masmoudi said. "You know how it is with these young men these days. Nothing but long hair and rebellion."

"Funny talk coming from a Marxist."

"Ah, but then we have the only true answer," he said. "Everything else has been tried."

It was a superbly arrogant remark and delivered with a smile of considerable charm so that I didn't know whether to take him seriously or not.

He patted the divan beside him and said to Simone, "A glass of champagne while we're waiting."

"I'd rather have a brandy." For the first time I noticed that she was trembling slightly.

He stood up, quite unconcerned, went to a cupboard in one corner, produced a cut-glass decanter and a glass, filled it and brought it to her. She took it gratefully and thanked him.

He put a hand on her shoulder, "You are soaked to the skin, little flower. Permit me."

He moved to the closet into which Langley had pushed the whore, opened it, giving us a further brief glimpse of her, took out a military greatcoat with a sheepskin collar and closed the door again on the startled woman.

He held the coat open for Simone, a slight smile on his face, and she stood up, took off her wet burnous, and pulled it on. Again she smiled her gratitude.

"Heh, I like that," Barzini said, and he helped himself to the brandy. "He knows how to treat a lady. He's been well brought up."

I was aware of a vague irrational annoyance. The whole thing was really becoming quite farcical, and then there was the rasp of feet on the terrace outside and a knock on the door.

Everyone scattered, taking up positions quickly and I nodded to Masmoudi. He called out in Arabic. The door opened and a prisoner in striped cotton pajamas and leg irons was propelled into the room with such force that he fell on his knees. The sergeant who moved in behind him was an enormous black-bearded man and I knew this must be Husseini.

Nino kicked the door shut and rammed the muzzle of his AK into Husseini's ribs and I reached over and lifted the service revolver from his holster. Like his master, he showed no great emotion. A dour, implacable man who took in the situation calmly and clasped his hands behind his neck when Langley told him to.

The man in the striped pajamas was in a bad way and had obviously recently had a severe beating. His right cheek was split so that it really required two or three stitches and a nasty green bruise ran up into the eye.

I dropped to one knee beside him. "Stephen Wyatt?"

"That's right." His voice was hoarse and broken and he appeared dazed. More than that, there was genuine fear in his eyes.

"It's all right," I said. "You've nothing to worry about. Not any more. We've come to get you out."

"Out?" he said slowly. "Out of prison, you mean? I don't understand."

It was as if everything about him, each sense, had been dulled at the edges. I said, "You don't need to," and I looked up at Masmoudi. "Let's have these leg irons off."

He gave Husseini a brief order in Arabic and the big sergeant produced a key and leaned down to take off the irons. Wyatt shrank away from him which told its own story. I pulled him to his feet and he stood there, swaying, a look of complete bafflement on his face.

I said to Masmoudi, "Right, we're going to leave now. Tell Husseini to help the boy across the square. We all leave in the one truck. You drive, Aldo. I'll sit up front with you and we'll have the colonel between us. The rest of you in the back." I turned again to Masmoudi. "You're going to take us straight through the front gate. Understand?"

"Perfectly."

He spoke again in Arabic to Husseini who, dour as ever, showed no emotion, but simply got an arm round Wyatt and moved to the door. Nino opened it for them, I stood back and motioned Masmoudi and Simone through and the rest of us followed.

It was still raining as we went down the path. Husseini opened the gate and started through with Wyatt; Masmoudi stood to one side for Simone. "After you, little flower."

She smiled in spite of herself, moving to pass him, and with a courtly smile still on his lips, he pushed her into me with all his force, jumped into the bushes and ran like hell, calling to Husseini at the same time. Wyatt came staggering back through the gate and Husseini took off across the square, zig-zagging furiously to avoid the possibility of a bullet in the back.

Not that there seemed much point. I grabbed Wyatt by one arm, "Right, make for those trucks while there's still time."

I was kidding myself, of course, for as we ran out of the gate and started across the square, four or five soldiers rushed out of the guardroom by the main gate.

There was a certain amount of confusion which was understandable enough when one considers that we must have looked at first sight like a group of their own comrades. And then Husseini dodged out of the shadows, yelling in Arabic and the fat was in the fire.

The nearest one to us loosed off a burst of his assault rifle on full automatic, firing from the hip a yard wide of us to the right, the bullets ricocheting from the cobbles. Hampered by Wyatt, who was leaning heavily on me, there wasn't a great deal I could do in return, but someone fired three or four shots from behind me that lifted the soldier right off his feet, slamming him back against one of the trucks.

His comrades retreated, firing wildly, and Langley and Nino both replied with long bursts that drove them back into the shelter of the parked trucks. Which left us still completely exposed. The sentry above the gate fired twice and far too close for comfort so I drew the Stechkin machine pistol I carried on my right hip from its wooden holster. As I'd set it on full automatic he got about fifteen rounds in reply for one pull of the trigger and fell off the wall into the entrance to the gateway tunnel.

Barzini grabbed Wyatt's other arm and we ran for the train, dragging him between us, Simone at our heels. We dropped him in the shelter of the first boxcar and Langley and Nino joined us, both firing short bursts from the hip to cover our retreat.

I crouched beside the track and peered through one of the wheels. It was a mess, no doubt about that. Soldiers appearing as if by magic from all over the place, some of them only half dressed, but all with rifles in their hands.

Bullets thudded into the boxcar and ricocheted from the wheels. Langley appeared beside me, grinning like a fiend. "Not so good, old stick. The best laid schemes, eh?"

A bullet clipped the woodwork just above his head, a splinter slicing his cheek like a razor. He put his fingers to it and looked at the blood and stopped smiling just like that.

"Bastards!" he said. "Bloody wog bastards! I'll give them something to think about."

He pulled one of the Sturma stick grenades from his belt, yanked the pin and lobbed it over the top of the boxcar towards the gate area. It landed on one of the trucks and fell between two of them. Someone cried out in alarm and several soldiers ran into the open. Langley jumped out of cover himself, laughing insanely and cut three of them down, firing from the hip.

A second later the grenade exploded, blowing one truck onto its side and then, like an instantaneous echo, its petrol tank went up, scattering chunks of metal, wood and burning debris far across the courtyard.

It was a scene from hell, flames everywhere, soldiers searching helplessly for cover, Langley and Nino firing steadily. A half naked woman staggered across the courtyard, screaming, and fell over a body. Husseini ran out of the shelter of the gateway to get her, firing a submachine gun with one hand. I could have shot him, but held my fire. He was a brave man, whatever else he was.

A bullet tugged at my left shoulder and then a whole stream ripped into the boxcar above our heads. When I turned, Masmoudi was in the gateway of the house firing an AK at us and two men beside him were setting up a light machine gun on its tripod.

Barzini pulled at my sleeve. "We stay here, we're finished. Better inside."

We got Wyatt on his feet again, dazed and uncomprehending, and ran alongside the train into the engine shed. Simone and Nino were right behind us, but Langley was taking his own sweet time, firing madly. It was only when the light machine gun opened up that he turned and ran for it.

I eased Wyatt down against the wall beside the locomotive. It was warm up there. There was a smell of hot iron and steam. I turned to Simone. "Are you all right?"

She nodded. "What are we going to do, Oliver?"

"God knows." I looked around me. The shed was partially illuminated by the flickering light from the burning tracks. "This certainly looks like a dead enough end."

Langley was crouched at the entrance, peering outside. For a moment there seemed a lull in the firing. I said, "What's going on out there?"

"I think he's grouping his forces, old stick. Better get ready for some sort of frontal assault."

Nino called, "Look what I found. A machine gun."

It was mounted on the roof of the boxcar immediately behind the engine tender. Like the rest of their hardware it was Russian, an RPD using hundred-round dram magazines. There were about eight of those in the ammunition box beside it. Which was something because the way things were shaping up we'd need all the help we could get.

I jumped down and joined Langley at the entrance. Over by the tracks a line of men were trying to do something about the fire, passing buckets of water from hand to hand. Masmoudi had thirty or forty men beside the villa wall and he and Husseini had their heads together.

"What do you think?" Langley said.

I didn't get a chance to reply because there was a sudden sharp cry behind me and Barzini called, "Heh, Oliver, look at this."

He had climbed up into the cab of the locomotive and now appeared holding a tiny wizened little Arab in greasy khaki turban and bush shirt.

"He was hiding up here."

The little Arab said, "No, effendi, please. I meant no harm. I am the engine driver. Talif."

"You speak good English," I said.

"Damn good English, effendi. I work for British army during the war. I served with General Montgomery."

Somehow he made it sound personal. I said, "What were you doing up there?"

"Sleeping, effendi. It's warm next to the fire box and then the shooting started ... I was afraid."

I said, "There's a fire going in this thing?"

"But of course, effendi. We leave at seven in the morning on the Tripoli run and without steam ..."

Langley, who had been listening from the entrance, said, "Do you mean you've got a head of steam on?" He kicked a wheel. "Will she go?"

"You mean now, effendi?" Talif shrugged. "Not at full power, you understand. For that the fire would need stoking."

"How fast?" I demanded impatiently.

"Fifteen, maybe twenty miles an hour."

Barzini said, "You think this could be our way out, Oliver?"

"It's got to be. The only question is can the damn thing move fast enough to take that gate with it."

"There's only one way to find out." He turned to Nino. "Heh, boy, you get in that cab and start shoveling coal. I want to hear that fire roar."

Nino did as he was told and Talif said timidly, plucking at my sleeve, "You are taking the train, effendi?"

"No, you are," I said. "We're just coming along for the ride."

"Please—effendi." He looked scared to death. "On my mother's grave, I beg you. Colonel Masmoudi will hang me up by my ears if I should do such a thing."

"And if you don't," Barzini told him, cheerfully, "I'll hang you up by something else. Now climb in that cab and get things started."

Talif turned away, shoulders hunched and scrambled up onto the footplate. I reached down and pulled Wyatt to his feet. He swayed, leaning against me, looking really ill.

"When do I wake up?" he said wearily. "Or don't you ever feel like that?"

"Only on Monday through Friday," I said and heaved back the sliding door of the boxcar with the machine gun on the top. "Just get in there and keep your head down." I gave him a push up and said to Simone, "You stay with him. All right?"

"He's in a bad way," she said.

"Aren't we all?"

"Now there speaks the hard-nosed bastard I've come to know and love," she said, and climbed up into the boxcar.

Langley was back at the entrance and now he called, "Better come quick, old stick. This looks interesting."

Masmoudi was half-way across the square waving a white handkerchief. Barzini said, "What do you think, Oliver?"

"I think you make ready to get out of here while I talk with our friend," I said and I shouldered my assault rifle and stepped into the open.

I went only a few yards in his direction then paused to light a cigarette, making him come the rest of the way. He smiled. "I like that. Nice and casual. Not a care in the world. Good psychology."

"You seem to know your business yourself," I said, more to keep the conversation going than anything else.

"I went to Sandhurst," he said simply.

Which was enough to take the wind out of anyone's sails. We stood facing each other against the backdrop of burning trucks looking, I suspect, faintly ridiculous. The assault group, under Husseini, crouched in the shelter of the wall. It had stopped raining and the sky was clearing fast.

I said, "What do you want?"

"I should have thought that was obvious. You are finished, you and your friends. You have failed. Why waste more lives? Better to give up now."

"And end like Wyatt? No, thanks."

"You are being very foolish," he said. "You cannot hope to last for long if I mount a general assault. At least let the girl leave."

"All right," I said. "I'll see what she says. Wait here."

I went back inside the engine shed. Nino was shoveling away for dear life and the smell of steam was heavy and pungent on the night air.

"What does he want?" Barzini demanded.

"Total surrender. Are we ready to go?"

He turned to Talif. "Well?"

Talif shrugged fatalistically. "As Allah wills, effendi. If you wish it, we go now, but as I warned you, we will be short of full power."

"Right, make ready and when I say go, you'd better get us out of here just as fast as you can because if we don't break that gate down at the first try, you're going to be just as much in trouble as the rest of us." I turned to the others. "I want one of you on top with that machine gun and really pour it on as we go across the square. Keep their heads down because that's going to be the crucial bit."

"Leave it to me, old stick." Langley climbed the ladder to the roof of the boxcar.

I nodded to Barzini who scrambled up onto the footplate. "All right, Aldo. When I say go, go."

I went out into the courtyard again where Masmoudi waited patiently. I said, "Sorry, she says she liked the champagne, but not the company."

"What a pity. On her own head be it then."

He turned and started to walk away and I hurried back inside the engine shed. "Okay, let's go, let's go!" I cried and I scrambled up into the boxcar beside Simone and Wyatt.

There was a hissing of steam, it billowed around the wheels as they started to turn, the clanging echoing between the brick walls. There was another great rush of steam, the wheels spun and then, quite suddenly, we coasted out into the open.

Masmoudi was only half way back to his men. He turned with a startled cry and raised an arm, calling on them, I suppose, to fire. He was in the way, which didn't help, but by then Langley was firing the machine gun, working it from side to side, knocking down several of the assault group and throwing the rest into complete confusion.

We were moving faster now, gliding across the square at perhaps ten miles an hour. Bullets started to fly when we were halfway across. I fired back from the entrance to the boxcar and behind me, Barzini and Nino were shooting from the footplate.

And then the first cars were inside the tunnel and I shouted to Simone. "Hang on tight, this could be rough."

There was a great splintering crash, the boxcar rocked from side to side. For the briefest of moments we seemed to stand still and then nudged inexorably onwards, the great double gates falling to each side, torn from their hinges.

We moved on, wheels rattling over the points to a chorus of angry shouts and a great deal of shooting, none of which did any good at all, for a moment later we really started to pick up speed and were away.

CHAPTER TWELVE

Night Run

THE SKY HAD CLEARED CONSIDERABLY BY now and the moon was very bright, stars strung away to the horizon. Barzini leaned out of the cab and called, "Heh, we showed them, didn't we, Oliver?"

"I'm coming over." I turned to Simone. "How are you doing?"

"Fine. I'm not too sure about Wyatt. He seems very weak to me. They must have given him a terrible time in there."

He lay back, his head on her lap, eyes closed. I said, "All right, do what you can. I'll be back."

I left the assault rifle beside her and worked my way along the side of the boxcar, hanging on to the bars until I reached the tender. From there it was an easy matter to make it to the footplate.

The fire was roaring. Nino shoveling away, covered in sweat, but we were still doing no more than fifteen miles an hour. I said to Talif, "How close do we go to Gela?"

"Half a mile, effendi. No more. There is a tunnel there. Maybe a fifteen-mile run from here."

"Fifteen miles?" Barzini said. "You must be crazy. It's not half that."

"As the crow flies, effendi, but the line loops inland for some distance. It was the easiest way to lay track when the Italians built it."

"So it gets us there what does it matter?" Nino said. "Half an hour ago we were dead men." He laughed out loud and tossed a piece of coal out into the night. "Do you suppose Lazarus felt like this?"

"Don't look now," Barzini said, "but I think someone just threw another spadeful of earth on the lid of your coffin."

I turned to look where he pointed. At that place a road ran parallel to the track perhaps fifty yards away. Three Landrovers followed each other in echelon, each with a light machine gun mounted on a tripod. Masmoudi was in the front one with Husseini and three soldiers, clear in the moonlight.

The machine guns in the two rear Landrovers opened up. As Langley replied, Masmoudi's Landrover picked up speed and forged ahead, disappearing into the night at sixty or seventy miles an hour.

The two remaining Landrovers kept on firing and Langley replied with the RPD. They were scoring hits only occasionally for the road kept swinging away because of the terrain. After a few minutes we ran into an area of low hills studded with olive groves and lost them altogether.

"Do we meet the road again?" I asked Talif.

"Five or six miles from here, effendi."

"And how long does it stay with us?"

"A mile or two—no more. We come together again about five miles after that close to the Gela tunnel. The road stays with the railway then, except for the section through the cut as far as the river crossing. That's two miles further on."

I said to Barzini, "I'd better warn Langley," and I scrambled up over the tender to the top of the boxcar.

He was reloading as I joined him. "How's it going, old stick?"

I filled him in on the situation ahead. He seemed completely unconcerned and lit a cigarette. "Lovely night for it."

Crazy it may sound, but he was right. The sky was clear and bright, stars everywhere and the moon seemed bigger than I'd ever known it before, bathing the countryside in its hard, white light. The hills were like silhouettes cut out of black paper, the valleys and defiles between them very dark. We were picking up speed now and I left him and worked my way back over the tender to the cab.

I said, "So far so good. Things might warm up in another five or ten minutes, but the crunch is going to come when we reach the Gela tunnel."

Barzini stuck one of his Egyptian cheroots between his teeth. "If we simply stop the train and get off they'll see us. We won't last long on foot. Half a mile to the beach. They're certain to run us down."

"I'd been thinking about that one myself," I said. "Let's say the train stopped in the tunnel, time enough to get off, no more than that. If it came out at the other end with someone working the machine gun, they'd continue to follow. All the time in the world then to get Wyatt down to the beach."

"Heh," Nino said. "That makes a hell of a lot of sense to me."

"Except for the guy on the machine gun." Barzini prodded me in the shoulder angrily. "Naturally you see yourself in that heroic position. What's wrong with you? You got a death wish or something?"

"Not particularly," I said. "It's simple enough. I stay with the train for another couple of miles, probably until the river crossing, then jump for it. If I do it right, they'll still follow the train. I'll be in Gela inside the hour."

"And if you're not?"

"You put to sea. You carry on with the job. You get Wyatt back and exchange him for Hannah. Then you see she gets back to London safely, that's all I ask."

"On your own you don't stand a chance," Barzini said. "If you stay, I stay."

"Now who's talking like a crazy man? You've seen the state Wyatt's in. He wouldn't make fifty yards on his own. Getting him half a mile over rough country to that beach is going to take all of you."

"He's right," Nino said. "Face facts, Uncle Aldo."

Barzini knew it, but didn't like it. He turned away, stamping his feet angrily. I said to Nino, "Tell Langley and Simone. Make sure they know exactly what we're doing. When the time comes everybody's going to have to move fast."

He slung his rifle over his shoulder and worked his way along the bars to the entrance to the boxcar. Barzini jerked a thumb at Talif. "What about him? How can you guarantee he'll keep this thing rolling with no one to watch him?" He brightened suddenly. "On the other hand, it's the rails that take it where it's going. You only need the driver to turn it on and off."

The look of dismay on Talif's face was something to see, for I suppose he imagined a bullet in the head might be next on the agenda. "Effendi—please. I give my word. I swear on my mother's grave."

"No need," I said. "I prefer a business arrangement. Much more sensible."

In the past, I had always carried a little mad money with me on such assignments, just in case anything went drastically wrong and I'd seen no reason to alter the habit on this occasion, there being no difficulty in fulfilling my requirements in Palermo. I opened a canvas purse at the back of my webbing belt, took out a small leather bag and poured the contents into Talif's hand.

"The trouble with paper money is that it changes from country to country," I said. "But this kind of thing is welcomed everywhere. Gold pieces, my friend. English sovereigns. Fifty of them."

His eyes widened, the mouth opened in awe. For a long moment he stared down at them and then he quickly poured them back into the leather bag, tied it and stowed it carefully away in his tunic pocket.

"All right, effendi, I do it, but there is one thing more you must do for me."

"And what would that be?"

"Beat me, effendi." He pointed to his face. "Knock hell out of me so Colonel Masmoudi can see I didn't have any choice."

Barzini laughed harshly, "You know something, he's got a point."

Talif turned to him, smiling eagerly, and Barzini punched him in the mouth, grabbed him by the shirt front and punched him again. A third blow drove him to his knees and Barzini moved back.

Talif looked up, blood pouring from his smashed nose and lips. He touched his face gingerly with his fingertips and actually smiled as he stood up. "Excellent, effendi. Exactly what I wanted."

"A pleasure to do business with you," Barzini said, and at that moment Langley cried out a warning and there was a burst of firing.

I went up over the tender and found him on top of the boxcar. There was the road again, fifty or sixty yards away to the right. The two Landrovers emerged from an olive grove where they had presumably been waiting and drove on a parallel course, their machine guns working furiously.

They were scoring plenty of hits on the boxcars but nothing serious and Langley was giving it to them good and hot in return. He ran out of ammunition and I yanked off the empty and shoved on another hundred round drum for him as the Landrovers disappeared into a fold in the ground.

"Now you see them, now you don't," he shouted. "I used to be great at this sort of thing in the amusement arcades on the front at Brighton. Nino tells me you intend to go out trailing clouds of glory?"

"I always fancied it," I said. "Like Beau Geste and his Viking funeral."

The Landrovers emerged into an open stretch of road again and commenced firing, bullets plowing into the top of the boxcar in front of us. Langley answered in a continuous burst that seemed to go on for ever and suddenly, the rear Landrover veered sharply off the road and plowed through an olive grove, coming to rest against a stone wall.

The other vanished from sight as the road disappeared behind a series of low hills and Langley laughed out loud and patted the RPD. "One down, one to go."

"Two to go," I said. "You're forgetting the lead Landrover—the one with Masmoudi and Husseini in it."

He looked mildly surprised, "You know, you've got a point there, old stick. What do you think they're up to?"

"Something nasty, I've no doubt. Maybe they intend to try and block the track at some suitable point up ahead. If they do, I'm keeping my fingers crossed it's after the Gela tunnel. That's our big strength. Masmoudi doesn't know where we intend to get off."

"I'll keep my eyes skinned," he said cheerfully. "I'd like to cut a notch for Masmoudi before we go."

I left him and climbed down the side of the boxcar, using the bars and slipped inside. Wyatt still lay with his head in Simone's lap and Nino crouched beside them.

"How is he?" I asked.

"Not so good," Nino answered. "I tell you something. Getting him down to the beach is going to be one hell of a job."

"I didn't say it would be easy." I dropped to one knee beside Simone. "You know what to do when we reach the tunnel?"

"Yes. Nino told me." She put a hand on my arm. "Has it got to be this way, Oliver?"

"Can you suggest anything better?" Her eyes dropped and I patted her cheek. "See you in church. Keep smiling."

She looked up. "Is that a promise?"

But I didn't reply to that one, mainly because there didn't really seem to be much point. I worked my way along the bars to the tender and joined Barzini on the footplate.

There was a quick burst of firing from Langley and I turned to see the remaining Landrover appear briefly in a gap between two hills. It didn't bother to reply and disappeared a moment later. This performance was repeated three or four times over the next couple of miles. It was somehow uncanny, the Landrover appearing and disappearing in the hard white light of the moon without a sound except for the sullen chatter of Langley's machine gun, the rattle of the train.

"What are they playing at?" Barzini demanded. "Why don't they fire?"

"Keeping us under observation, is my guess," I said. "They've got a radio aerial on that thing, which means they're probably giving Masmoudi a blow-by-blow account every step of the way."

"And where in the hell is Masmoudi?"

"Somewhere up ahead, waiting for us." I turned to Talif. "Where would be a good place?"

"To block the line, effendi? That's easy. There is a way station at Al Haifa on the other side of the river. There are points there and a loop so that we can be taken off the main line if something is coming the other way."

"I see," I said. "So he's no need to block the line, just throw the points and we'll be turned into that loop without being able to do a damn thing about it."

Barzini chuckled and slapped me on the back. "And the only thing wrong with that from Masmoudi's point of view, is that we'll be long gone."

"Gela tunnel very soon now, effendi," Talif said. "Other side of the next cut."

We dropped into a defile between high banks, came out of the other side at the top of a long incline and below, perhaps quarter of a mile away, was the entrance to the tunnel. There were olive groves on the left dropping down to the sea, clear in the moonlight. Langley loosed off a quick burst and I turned and saw the Landrover appear briefly on a clear section of road.

It disappeared and Talif was already applying the brakes as we coasted over the final section of track into the dark mouth of the tunnel. Once inside, he braked hard and we ground to a halt.

Steam seemed to be everywhere. Barzini jumped from the footplate and ran to the entrance of the boxcar to help Nino and Simone with Wyatt. Langley came down across the tender in a shower of coal. He said something before he jumped down to join the others but I couldn't hear it because of the hissing of the steam.

Barzini called, "Okay, we're clear!" I tapped Talif on the shoulder and we started to move again.

I opened the gate to the fire box and started to shovel coal and Talif pulled on the cord above his head and sounded the whistle, a banshee wail rebounding from one wall to the other.

"Good, effendi?" he shouted above the noise of the train.

"Very good!" I said.

I could see the other end of the tunnel now. I pushed in some more coal, kicked the door shut and threw down the shovel. As we coasted out into the fresh night air, Talif sounded the whistle again and it echoed far away across the valley.

"Thomas Wolfe would have approved of you," I said.

"Effendi?" He looked completely bewildered.

At that moment the Landrover appeared on a stretch of road to our right. I turned to scramble across the tender to reach the machine gun, too late, for it was already firing.

As I went over the top of the boxcar, the Landrover disappeared from view again and Langley turned from the RPD and grinned. "Ah, there you are, old stick."

"What in the hell are you doing here?" I demanded.

"Couldn't very well leave you to all those tedious heroics on your own," he said. "Two pairs of hands are better than one and all that sort of rubbish. Or it could just be that I've grown to care for you."

"What about Wyatt?"

"Barzini and Nino can manage him between them. I'd only have got in the way." He grinned and stuck a cigarette in his mouth. "Aren't you glad I'm on your side?"

It stank, of course, because whatever else he was there for, it wasn't for the good of my health, of that I was certain. If I'd had any sense, I'd have shot the bastard out of hand there and then, but there was a chance that we might still need each other so, for the moment, I decided to go along with the idea while making damn sure that I never turned my back on him.

The engine started to labor as we moved into the cut Talif had spoken of. It was very steep, the banks towering above us on each side.

"Over the hill and only two more miles to the river crossing," Talif shouted.

There was a dull thud on the roof of the cab. I leaned out on the footplate and saw Colonel Masmoudi dropping in on Langley from the top of the cut.

I turned to go up over the tender to Langley's assistance and Sergeant Husseini swung down from the roof of the cab through the other entrance and kicked me in the face. I should have gone straight out backwards and finished up under the wheels, but the instinctive response of the trained soldier had me already turning so that his boot only grazed my right cheek.

It was almost enough, for I did swing out into space for a moment, although I managed to grab one of the hand rails. I pulled myself in again in time to see Talif struggling in the sergeant's grip. He didn't stand a chance and Husseini simply threw him away from him. Talif grabbed for a rail, missed, and disappeared with a terrible cry.

Husseini was at the controls now, wrenching at the brake lever. I pulled out the Stechkin machine pistol awkwardly with my left hand because I was still hanging on to the grab rail with my right. Some instinct made him turn, eyes burning in that dark face, but by then it was too late. I shot him once in the right shoulder, the high velocity bullet turning him round in a circle. My second shot shattered his spine, driving him headfirst into darkness.

As I scrambled up across the tender, the machine gun went over with a crash. Langley and Masmoudi rolled from one side of the roof to the other, tearing at each other's throats like a couple of mad dogs, in imminent danger of falling over the edge to the track at any moment.

It was difficult to get a clear shot as they twisted and turned in the shadows, but in any event I had other things on my mind. The train came out of the cutting and breasted the hill and below, at the end of a two mile gradient was the bridge over the river.

Something else was unpleasantly clear also—the three soldiers in camouflaged uniforms working their way along the line of boxcars, obviously the rest of the crew of the lead Landrover.

I fired several shots to keep their heads down, but without much effect, for the train was picking up speed now on the slope, swaying like a crazy thing.

There was really only one sensible thing to do under the circumstances so I eased myself down between the tender and the boxcar and got to work on the coupling hook and chain. The retaining pin came out with surprising ease, but we all stayed together for the present, which was only to be expected on the downhill run.

I scrambled back over the tender to the cab, got a hand to the brake lever and turned. Langley and Masmoudi were on their feet now and face to face, and none of your nasty karate either. They squared up to each other like gentlemen, swapping punch for punch, but I suppose that was only to be expected when Eton met Sandhurst.

I fired a shot into the air and as Langley turned his head, yelled, "Jump for it! Your only chance!" Then I pulled down the brake lever.

He had the sense to obey me without question, leaping high into the air, landing in the tender's coal bunker as the gap widened and the rest of the train drew away rapidly downhill, Masmoudi standing at the edge of the boxcar, his men working their way towards him. And then he did a strange thing. He put his heels together and saluted.

"My God!" I said. "More English than the bloody English themselves. Branded clean to the bone; That's Sandhurst for you."

Langley picked up an assault rifle from the floor of the cab and took careful aim. I knocked up the barrel as he fired and the bullet soared into space.

"You'd shoot anything rather than nothing, wouldn't you?"

"Peck's bad boy, that's me," he replied amiably.

The engine had ground to a halt and the rest of the train plus Masmoudi and his men was quarter of a mile away down the grade now and moving fast. I fiddled around with the controls which were simple enough and finally got the wheels to turn again, but in the opposite direction this time.

We started to climb back up the grade and I told Langley to stand on top of the tender and keep his eyes peeled for the other Landrover, just in case it decided to reappear.

We went over the hill and started the long run down to the tunnel through the cut. I hadn't bothered reholstering the Stechkin, but held it in my right hand against my thigh. I didn't trust him, not for one single moment. Certainly if the idea was to put me out of the way for good and all, the present situation was made to order.

I positioned myself carefully, one eye on the controls, the other on him and as we neared the mouth of the tunnel, I hooked open the fire-box gate with one foot so that the flickering flames illuminated both the cab and general area of the tender. I think he knew what I was up to for there was a slight, amused smile on his mouth.

We coasted out on the other side of the tunnel and I shoved on the brakes to slow her up a little. "Get ready to jump!" I told him.

"Are you going to leave her running, old stick?"

"I don't see why not. That way they won't have the slightest idea where we got off. With any luck she'll keep right on going until she ends up back in that prison yard."

I jumped then, quite suddenly and without telling him, no great feat as the train was doing no more than ten miles an hour. I hit the gravel at the side of the track, still running and Langley followed, perhaps twenty or thirty yards further on. I scrambled up the banking quickly and was on top, ready and waiting as he arrived.

The train disappeared around a curve and Langley joined me. "There she goes, out of our lives forever. I feel quite sad. What now?"

"We make tracks," I said. "For Gela and as fast as we can. I told Barzini to give me an hour, remember, and then leave and he's just liable to take me at my word."

I was still holding the Stechkin, I let him see that and I waited, making him move out first which he did, although that same tiny amused smile was in evidence as if he knew what I was thinking and found the whole damn thing too funny for words.

But that didn't matter. Not as far as I was concerned. I had his back in front of me all the way down the hillside to the sea and that was all I was interested in.

I checked my watch as we went down through the olive grove on the outskirts of Gela. The Bedouin camp was quiet. A dog barked once at our passing, then subsided.

The general store was in darkness also, except for a single light on the veranda, but as we passed a voice hissed from the shadows, "Signor Grant! Over here!"

Izmir stood against the wall, concealed from view by a buttress. "What is it?" I said.

"Your friends are in bad trouble, signor. The customs launch and Lieutenant Ibrahim returned this evening after you had left and tied up at the pier."

"Did he visit the *Palmyra?*"

"Oh, yes, signor."

Which was a really bad break if you like and I wondered what Angelo had told him.

"Three of his men were up here very late, signor, drinking and playing cards. Someone came for them from the customs launch. It seems they had received a message over the radio asking them to check all strange boats. Something to do with an escape from Râs Kanai."

"Has anyone else come through here within the past half an hour or so?" I said.

"Your friends, signor. Lieutenant Ibrahim had them arrested at once and your boat brought in to the pier."

"That's bloody marvelous," Langley said. "I mean to say that really does make it the end of a perfect day."

"My thanks," I said to Izmir and moved off into the darkness toward the pier, and this time I didn't worry too much about my back because it struck me with some force that in the circumstances, Langley and I needed each other rather badly.

The customs launch was moored at the end of the pier and the *Palmyra* was tied up to her. The deck lights were turned on giving plenty of illumination.

Barzini, Nino, Simone, and Angelo stood together by the wheelhouse, all with their hands clasped behind their backs. Wyatt sat on the deck, his back to the rail.

Lieutenant Ibrahim confronted them, full of self importance. Six or seven sailors stood in a half circle, rifles at the ready.

We paused in the shelter of a beached fishing boat. "My God," Langley said, "they'll make him a Hero of the Revolution or something for this night's work. Flag rank at the very least. The thing is, what are we going to do about it?"

"Whatever it is, it had better be quick," I said. "I should think he's been on the radio to Tripoli by now. He doesn't strike me as the sort to hide his light under a bushel."

There was no one stationed at the RPD machine gun mounted on the swivel in the stern. I pointed it out to Langley. "Do you think you could swim round the end of the pier and take charge of that thing if I created a diversion?"

"I should imagine so."

"All right, off you go. I'll give you five minutes."

He dodged along the beach, keeping to the shadows and entered the water close to the pier itself. I watched very closely, could just see his head as he went round the end of the pier. It was then that I made my move.

I unclipped the Stechkin's wooden holster from my belt and clipped it into place, forming a shoulder stock. Then I took careful aim and shot out the launch's masthead light.

It was almost funny. Everybody went down including the sailors, except for Ibrahim, who drew a pistol. I fired again, shattering a window in his wheelhouse and three of his men fired wildly in my general direction. By that time I was flat on my face behind the boat and when I looked up again it was in time to see Langley haul himself over the rail behind them and take charge of the machine gun, swinging it on its swivel and firing a short burst out into the bay.

The effect was spectacular. Ibrahim and his men all turned and froze, trapped by this new menace. As I ran across the sand to the pier, Langley spoke to them in Arabic. The sailors turned uncertainly to look at Ibrahim and Langley loosed off another burst that shattered every window in the wheelhouse. This time everyone, including Ibrahim, did as they had obviously been told and threw their weapons over the side into the sea.

"Now we'll have them all on the pier," I said to Langley as I stepped over the rail.

He again gave them the necessary order and the sailors complied without hesitation. Ibrahim was slightly more reluctant and said to me, eyes smoldering, "You cannot hope to get away with this. The Libyan navy ..."

"What navy, for Christ's sake?" Barzini put a boot to his rear that sent him staggering over the rail.

"Right, let's get out of here," I said.

Nino and Barzini lifted Wyatt across the rail to the *Palmyra* and took him below and Simone went with them. I told Angelo to cast off, went into the wheel-house and started the engines. Barzini and Nino came back on deck holding assault rifles and stood at the rail covering the sailors.

"All right," I called to Langley. "Let's go."

He lifted the RPD off its tripod and threw it into the sea, then boarded *Palmyra* grinning hugely. "Anything else I can do for you, old stick?"

"Come to think of it, there is." I took one of the Sturma stick grenades from my belt and passed it out of the window to him. "You did a neat job on those tracks back at the prison. Let's see what you can accomplish this time."

"My pleasure."

As I increased power and turned *Palmyra* away he yanked the pin and stood at the rail holding the grenade for what seemed an inordinate length of time, only throwing it at the last possible moment. It sailed through one of the broken windows of the wheelhouse and exploded, with unfortunate consequences for Lieutenant Ibrahim and two of his men who were in the act of boarding.

The launch started to burn furiously and there was a further explosion when the fuel tank went up, but by that time I was taking *Palmyra* through the passage between the Sisters and out to sea fast.

CHAPTER THIRTEEN

REBEL WITHOUT
A CAUSE

I SWITCHED ON EVERY LIGHT WE had and told Nino and Barzini to rig the fishing nets from mast to stern again.

"Page eighty-three of my copy of Mao Tse Tung on Guerrilla Warfare," I told Barzini when he joined me in the wheelhouse. "When a fish wishes to hide, it finds a shoal of fish. He suggests the revolutionary does the same."

"Do we qualify?"

"Well, let's put it this way. There are a hell of a lot of tunny boats scattered around between here and an outer limit that varies between ten to fifteen miles. This way we look just like all the others, so if anyone is searching for us, good luck to them."

God knows why I felt so cheerful, but in any event, we were soon passing through the tunny fleet. It required some careful navigating and I had to keep a constant eye out for nets, but within an hour or so we were leaving their lights behind. I pushed the engines up to full power and pressed on into the darkness.

For most of the time I was alone, but finally Simone appeared with coffee and sandwiches. She put the tray on the chart table and I locked on to automatic steering.

"What happened back there on the train after we left?" she asked.

I told her. When I'd finished she said, "I'm glad you didn't shoot Masmoudi. He was rather nice. Not at all as that revolting little Zingari man described him."

"I see." I pulled her into my arms. "You fancied him, did you?"

"Very definitely," she said. "Only duty called."

"How's Wyatt?"

"Not so good. Barzini and Nino had to drag him every step of the way from the railway line to the beach. He should be in hospital, Oliver. He's a sick man."

"What's he doing now?"

"Sleeping. He was completely exhausted."

"Did he say anything?"

She shook her head. "Not a word. For most of the time he was conscious he just didn't seem to be able to take in what was happening. He's in the aft cabin."

"Okay," I said. "This is what I want you to do. Go back and stay with him. You use the other bunk. I don't want him left alone with Langley on any account. I'll join you later."

"But I don't understand," she said. "Why should Justin cause trouble now? It doesn't make sense."

"Sense or not, he's up to something. I've never been more certain of anything in my whole life, so you watch him."

She went out and I unlocked the automatic pilot and took the wheel again and sat back thinking about it all. What could Langley be up to? It was a puzzle certainly. Possibly Stephen Wyatt could provide some answers.

The door banged open and Barzini entered. "I'll take over. You get some sleep."

"I've told Simone to stay with Wyatt. I think I'll bunk in with her."

"You expecting trouble?"

"From Langley?" I shrugged. "God knows, but I don't trust that character an inch. Better to be safe than sorry. You watch yourself, too, understand?"

He took a .38 Smith and Wesson from his pocket and laid it to hand on the chart table. "I got a friend. No need to worry about me, so off you go."

When I went down into the saloon Langley was stretched out on one of the bench seats smoking a cigarette. He glanced up and smiled. "Looking for me, old stick?"

For a moment I was tempted to have it out with him, but have what out, that was the trouble. I could see his bland smile now. The simulated bewilderment.

"Not particularly," I said and I opened the door to the aft cabin and went inside.

I bolted it behind me. Simone was in one bunk, a blanket draped round her shoulders, and Wyatt was in the other. She wasn't sleeping, but Wyatt was dead to the world, the bruised face tired and full of strain.

I took off my ammunition belt and placed it with the two Sturma grenades on top of the locker. Then I took off my boots and climbed into the bunk beside Simone pulling the blanket over both of us.

She snuggled into me, my arm about her. "This is nice."

What she didn't see was the Stechkin ready in my left hand under the blanket. Not that it mattered, for after a while she began to breathe slowly and steadily and I knew she was asleep.

One moment I was asleep and then awake, everything crystal clear and sharp. Simone was still dead to the world, her back toward me, but when I turned, Wyatt was lying on his side watching me. His left arm hung down to the floor and he was holding one of the stick grenades. He was still very pale and the bruising on his face looked ghastly, but a lot of the strain had gone. He seemed himself again, if I can put it that way, although that was obviously only an impression.

I said, "A nasty little toy if it's handled the wrong way."

He glanced down at the Sturma and frowned as if surprised to find it there. Then he put it down on top of the locker. "Who are you?"

There was a knock at the door and Barzini called, "Open up in there. It's coffee time. You having an orgy or something?"

As I got up to open the door, Simone awakened and stretched her arms. Barzini entered with a coffee pot in one hand and several cups in the other. "We're fresh out of cream," he said. "You'll have to drink it black and like it."

It was certainly strong enough and had the effect of a shot in the arm. "Where's Langley?" I said.

"Took over the wheel twenty minutes ago. Winds four to five with rain squalls. Bit of a sea running, but nothing to write home about."

Wyatt was sitting up, drinking his coffee, eyes watchful. I said, "How do you feel now?"

He came straight to the point. "Who in the hell are you? What is all this?"

"My name's Grant," I said. "This is Aldo Barzini and Simone Delmas. Your father sent us to get you out."

A look of complete astonishment appeared on his face. "My father?"

"Dimitri Stavrou."

"Oh, him." He leaned back against the bulkhead and laughed weakly. "So that's it? So it is just a dream after all." He looked me straight in the face and said calmly, "All right, Mr. Grant, how did he tell you to dispose of me? A bullet in the back of the skull? A knife in the ribs?"

I stared at him in astonishment and then some sort of light began to dawn. Simone said, "What's he talking about, Oliver?"

I'd pushed the Stechkin into my belt earlier. When I took it out Wyatt flinched, expecting the worst. Instead, I turned it butt first and put it into his hand.

"There's the safety catch," I said. "All right? Now I'll make a bargain with you. I'll tell you my side then you tell me yours. I've an idea we're both in for a surprise."

He fingered the Stechkin, a frown on his face, then said slowly, "Fair enough."

I said, "You were in Viet Nam?"

"That's right—paratroops, only don't start waving any flags."

"So was I for a while, among other things. I had a reputation for being able to get people out of places. People like you. Later, in civilian life, I made quite a living out of it."

"I get it. My stepfather hired you?"

"Not exactly. He tried to, but I'd decided to retire from the game. I wasn't interested."

"So how did he persuade you to change your mind?"

I told him in a few crisp, uncomplicated sentences. When I finished his face was bleak. "Typical of the bastard," he said. "The kind of nastiness he's been famous for all his life."

I said, "Al Capone must have loved him."

"I know one person who didn't. My mother. He treated her like a dog, Mr. Grant, for years. Used her only to further his own ends. She lived in total terror of him until the day she died. Trembled at the sound of his voice."

"But he told me he loved her," Simone said. "That was why he wanted you out of Râs Kanai. He looked upon it as some sort of sacred duty."

Wyatt laughed again. "He really does get better and better. When I got back from Nam I returned to Yale for a while, but it wasn't my scene anymore. You know how it is? I bummed around the Mediterranean for a while and then got mixed up with some Libyan students who didn't like the Quadhafi regime. The rest, as they say, is history."

"And your stepfather, he tried to get you released?" Barzini asked.

"Oh, sure." Wyatt was getting angry now. "But not because he wanted to do me any favor. That man wouldn't have sent flowers to my funeral. He hated my guts because I'd told him where he stood in my book on several occasions, some of them public. He only became interested in my welfare after my mother's death."

"I don't follow," I said.

"It's really quite simple. Like one of those big insurance policies, I'm worth more dead than alive, at least as far as my stepfather is concerned. You see, when he ran into trouble in the States and was deported, my mother was still left with her rights because she was American-born. So, he put everything in her name, and I mean everything. From a financial point of view a very lucrative thing to do under the circumstances. No risk to it, after all. As I've said, she was terrified of him. When he snapped his fingers she'd crawl."

"Heh, I'm beginning to see a little light here," Barzini cut in. "She decided to get her own back."

"That's it. She had cancer. She knew she was going so she had a will drawn up privately leaving the whole thing to me. Unfortunately, under the trust laws, I don't inherit till my twenty-fifth birthday and that isn't until next year."

"And if you die before then?" Simone said.

"Everything legally reverts to Dimitri—no problems." He chuckled. "God, but I'd have liked to have been there when the lawyers told him what she'd done. They say he was like a madman for three days."

"How long ago was this?" I said.

"About nine months."

I said to Simone, "And you knew nothing about this?"

"Not a word, I swear it," she said. "I was only with him for six months, remember."

Wyatt carried on. "He tried to get me to go and see him, made all sorts of promises, but I wasn't having any. Then somebody took a shot at me one night. I was still at Yale then. I figured there was a contract out on me and started running."

"Which was why you came to the Mediterranean? To hide?"

"I know, don't tell me. I certainly chose one hell of a public way of doing it. Face on the front page of every newspaper in the world. Show trial in Tripoli." He shook his head. "It's kind of funny when you look at it. When he finally found me I was as far off as ever."

There was a heavy silence as we all sat there thinking about it. Finally, I said, "If you made it to that twenty-fifth birthday of yours, what would you do?"

"Well, I'll tell you," he said. "That money was screwed out of people. Prostitution, drugs, protection —you name it and he had a finger in it, no matter how rotten. It seems to me that it would be kind of appropriate if it went back to people in some way. I know several relief organizations who could do one hell of a lot with five million dollars."

Simone's breath hissed between her teeth sharply. Barzini said with a kind of awe in his voice, "How much did you say?"

"Give or take a few bucks."

There was another long silence. Simone looked at me, I turned away, stood up and lit a cigarette. "Oliver?" she said.

"You're going to hand me over anyway, aren't you, Mr. Grant?" Wyatt's face was calm and one corner of his mouth lifted in a slight, ironic smile.

I turned, my back to the door. "What else can I do? He has my sister."

Simone plucked at my sleeve and I turned on her savagely. "The purpose of the exercise wasn't to take sides, it was to save Hannah. You know that as well as I do."

"You're living in a fool's paradise, Mr. Grant," Wyatt said. "You won't get your sister back. He never intended it All he wants is me—dead. Do you know what a truly evil man is?"

Barzini said, "I think maybe it's time we put Langley under wrappers."

"A good point," I said. "Any further discussion can come later."

"Who's Langley?" Wyatt asked me.

"Let's say he plays for the other team." I took the Stechkin from him and stuck it in my belt. "Sorry to be an Indian giver, but I've an idea I'm going to be needing this. You stay with him, Simone."

I opened the door and went out, followed by Barzini. The saloon was deserted and Barzini called, "Heh, Nino, where are you?"

"In here," Angelo replied from the forrard cabin.

The door was slightly ajar. I pushed it open and found Nino on the floor, hands lashed together, mouth taped, eyes blazing. Angelo slipped from behind the door and rammed the muzzle of an Uzi sub-machine gun under my chin.

"One move out of you, buster, and I'll blow the top of your head off."

He took the Stechkin from my belt and stuck it into his hip pocket then got a handful of hair and twisted me round, still keeping the muzzle of the Uzi tight under my chin.

Aldo had the Smith and Wesson in his hand. Angelo said, "Put it on the table slowly or he gets it. I'll only tell you once."

"I'd do as he says if I were you." Langley spoke from the companionway. He stepped in holding a revolver and plucked the Smith and Wesson from Barzini's hand. "That aft cabin ventilator's as good as a voice pipe, old stick," he told me. "You're slipping, aren't you, or perhaps you never really had it in the first place?"

"Bastard!" Barzini said to Angelo and spat on the floor.

"Oh, I don't know," Langley said. "He has his points. Hates my guts, but he does like the money in large amounts. Thirty thousand dollars, for example, as opposed to the twenty you were offering."

"Nothing personal," Angelo said. "I mean, I think you're a great guy, major, and all that, but like I said when we first met, I never did have much in common with officers."

Simone opened the door of the aft cabin and stepped into the saloon. She showed no kind of surprise at the situation. Her face was perfectly calm.

Langley said, "Ah, there you are, sweetie. How's our friend?"

"Not too good," she said, "but he'll survive."

"Do you really think so?" Langley chuckled. "All right, let's have him out of his bunk."

"You bloody lying bitch," I said.

She looked me over calmly, almost casually, a hand on one hip, no emotion in her eyes at all, then turned and went into the cabin.

"Put not thy trust in women, old stick." Langley sighed heavily. "My word, you really do have a lot to learn, don't you?"

"And what happens to Wyatt?" I said. "Over the side with sixty pounds of chain around his ankles?"

"You know, I'm beginning to despair of you." Langley leaned against the bulkhead casually. "I mean, he has to be identified, doesn't he, by competent witnesses so a Sicilian coroner can certify that Stephen Wyatt is beyond any shadow of a doubt legally deceased? Badly wounded while escaping from prison in Libya—died on the voyage back. Rather good that, don't you think?"

"And the rest of us?"

"It was carnage, old stick. Absolute bloodbath. A miracle any of us escaped with our lives."

"Just you and Angelo?"

"I should imagine so."

"Why bother?" I said. "I mean at thirty thousand dollars he comes expensive. Much cheaper to dump him too."

Angelo delivered a punch to my right kidney very expertly indeed. The pain was exquisite and I went down on one knee, fighting to control it. He raised a boot and Langley said sharply, "Leave it! Let's get this over with. I'm tired of conversation. Everyone on deck."

Wyatt shuffled out of the aft cabin leaning on Simone's shoulder. He looked at me questioningly as I hauled myself up by the table. "I'm sorry," I croaked. "Looks like the other team made it after all."

"Never mind," he said. "Morning soon and I'll wake up. Cell seventy-three, landing D."

Langley stepped back and said to Angelo, "Right, you first and stop the engines when you get up there." He nodded to Barzini, "You help Wyatt—all right? Then you, old stick, and nothing heroic, please, I do like to keep things tidy."

It was difficult for Barzini in the narrow companionway, especially when the engines stopped and *Palmyra* started to wallow, rolling heavily. Wyatt faltered and Langley shouted, "Go on, get moving, for God's sake!" They reached the deck safely and he waved his gun at me. "Now you."

I brushed past Simone as I moved forward, her fingers touched me quite deliberately—or did they? I couldn't be sure, but at least I went up the companion-way prepared for action, in spite of the terrible ache in my back.

It was raining hard, a cold wind lifting the waves into whitecaps and the deck seemed to be heaving in several directions at once. Angelo leaned against the wheelhouse covering Wyatt, who had slumped to the deck, and Barzini, who stood over him.

Langley waited until I had stepped out of the companionway before coming up followed by Simone. He kept his distance, cautious to the end. "Well now, how would you like it, old stick?" he said cheerfully.

Simone screamed, "Now, Oliver!" and grabbed his arms from behind.

But he already had a foot out to stamp in my chest as I jumped at him, sending me staggering back against the main hatch cover.

What really spoiled things was Angelo and all that Green Beret training because without a second's hesitation he clubbed Barzini over the back of the head with the Uzi. As Barzini went down, Wyatt grabbed Angelo's legs, trying to bring him over, and Angelo shot him in the body at close quarters.

Simone was still hanging on like a wild cat. Langley loosed off a shot into the deck then managed to get an elbow free and rammed it into her face, sending her flying. It was enough and as he swung to face me, the gun coming up, I took a very graceful header over the port rail.

I hit the water awkwardly and didn't have time to take in much air, but kept on going, turning to pass under the hull. The keel scraped my back painfully. For a moment I seemed to stop right there, lungs bursting, but I kicked and struggled for all I was worth and finally surfaced on the starboard side of *Palmyra*.

"Any sign of him?" I heard Langley call.

"He's had it," Angelo replied. "Must have done."

There was the sound of a slap. "You bloody bitch!" Langley said. "Couldn't stand to see him go when it came to the crunch, could you? I'll teach you." There was another heavy slap and Simone cried out.

I was bitterly cold and the pain in my back was excruciating, but hate has its own kind of strength and of one thing I was certain. I was going to get that bastard if it was the last thing I did on top of this earth.

I took a deep breath, hauled myself under the rail and started to crawl for the wheelhouse entrance.

"Ah, there you are, old stick," Langley called.

I glanced up instinctively and found him standing in the stern by the starboard rail. He fired twice from the waist, almost casually, and one of the bullets caught me in the right leg, knocking me over. I kept on going, scrambling into the wheelhouse, but he ran along the deck very quickly and stood in the doorway before I could reach what I was looking for.

I hung on to the open window to stop myself from falling down. He smiled gently and lowered the revolver, holding it against his thigh. "You don't look too good, old stick."

I was taking the greatest chance of my life, but I knew then with absolute certainty that there was only one way to handle it. To play to his vanity, that warped sense of humor. I scrabbled at the bulkhead as if trying to hold myself up, then pulled down the flap, grabbed the Uzi and turned, firing.

There was a series of dull clicks and Langley laughed delightedly. "Life's just full of surprises, isn't it? What a pity your girlfriend told me about that before her conscience started playing her up. Never mind. I'll see to her manners for her. Think about that in hell, won't you?"

I dropped the Uzi and slid down the bulkhead to the floor, my face a mask of despair. Langley was obviously thoroughly enjoying himself. He said, "Yes, you really look your age today, old stick. Definitely a tiny bit passé."

As he put a cigarette in his mouth my right hand found the button under the chart table, the flap fell, I grabbed the Stechkin and shot him through the right forearm, all in one quick movement. And part of the whole was wondering whether the thing would fire—whether Simone had been true to me.

The revolver dropped from his nerveless fingers, skidded across the swaying deck and under the rail into the sea. He clutched his arm, blood pouring between the fingers, that slight, fixed smile still in place.

"Lesson number one," I said. "If you're going to shoot somebody, do it, don't just talk about it."

"Well, I'll be damned," he said.

"I should think that's a cold, stone certainty," I told him. "Goodbye, *old stick!*"

I shot him in the left shoulder, turning him around, an echo of Husseini. The other two bullets shattered his spine, driving him across the starboard rail to land head-down. I crawled out of the wheelhouse, got him by the ankles with one hand, and tipped him over into the sea.

Angelo called, "Langley, you okay?"

I pulled myself along the deck by the starboard rail, dragging my wounded leg and he called out again, a certain amount of anxiety in his voice. "Heh, Langley—where are you?" And then he said impatiently, "For Christ's sake, be still or I'll crown you."

I pulled myself up on to my feet and stepped into the open. He was over by the port rail, his back partially turned to me, Simone held close to him, an arm around her neck, the Uzi ready in his other hand.

I extended my right arm and took very careful aim. "All right, Angelo, let her go."

He glanced over his shoulder and I cried savagely, "Now, not tomorrow!"

"Okay, man! Hold on to your cool!" He pushed her away from him. He started to turn and I saw his finger tighten on the trigger. "Let's talk this over. I'm willing to play along. You can trust me."

"Tell that to Langley," I said and fired.

He went down on one knee, dropping the Uzi. *God, but I was tired.* I grabbed at one of the wheelhouse windows to stop myself from falling down. He tried to reach for the Uzi, the *Palmyra* rolled very heavily and he lost his balance and skidded across the wet, sloping deck. He managed to grab the rail with one hand as he went under and hung there a moment glaring up at me, blood on his mouth. And then he could hang on to life no longer, released his grip and the gray sea closed over his head.

I let myself slide down to the deck and Simone dropped on her knees beside me, her eyes wild. "You did me fine," I said. "Beautiful! Go to the head of the class!"

There was a certain amount of blood soaking through my camouflaged trousers just above the knee. She started to examine it and I shook my head, "Never mind me. See to Wyatt."

He was lying on his face by the main hatch, Barzini crouched beside him shaking his head slowly, a dazed look in his eyes. He got to his feet, picked up a canvas bucket and line that hung by the wheelhouse and heaved it over the side. He emptied the bucket of ice cold water over his head and repeated the process.

Simone turned from her examination of Wyatt, her face grave. "It doesn't look too good."

Barzini said, "Here, let me see." He knelt beside her and opened Wyatt's pajama jacket. He turned, shaking his head. "He's been shot in the left lung. Probably grazed the heart on the way through. It's bad."

"How bad?"

"He could be dying, if that's what you mean." He told Simone to go and release Nino and came and knelt by me. "Let's have a look at you."

There was a nasty gash at the back of his head, blood on his forehead. I said, "Are you all right, Aldo?"

"What do you think? How did Langley look when you gave it to him?"

"Surprised."

"There's one man I'll find it difficult to remember in my prayers."

He ripped open the leg of my trousers and I raised my knee and had a look at the damage. There was the usual ragged blue hole where it had entered on the outside of the thigh just above the knee, a larger one on the inside where it had exited.

"A flea bite," Barzini said. "Three or four stitches and you'll be fine. I'll see to it personally."

"Just remember I'm not one of your damned corpses."

As he helped me to my feet, Nino came out of the companionway. "That stinking dirty pig," he said angrily. "He never even gave me a chance."

"Never mind that now," Barzini told him. "Let's get Oliver below."

They helped me down the companionway and put me on one of the bench seats in the saloon then they went back for Wyatt and took him into the aft cabin. Simone poured brandy into a mug and lit a cigarette for me.

"Now there's a nice intimate gesture," I told her.

She held the mug to my mouth, but I was suddenly shaking so much that half of it trickled over my chin and down my neck.

"Are you all right?" she asked, full of concern.

"Reaction. You don't feel a bullet when it hits you, not for quite a while because the shock numbs the whole nervous system. The pain comes later."

At that precise moment my leg began to hurt like hell and Barzini came in from the aft cabin holding the medicine chest. "No blood at all," he said. "All internal, I've bandaged him up and given him a morphine shot. There's nothing more I can do."

"Is he conscious?"

He nodded and said to Simone, "I think maybe he could do with a hot drink."

She went out and he propped my leg up on the table. He stuck a couple of ampoules of morphine into me for a start and then got to work with a needle and thread.

"My old granny would be proud of you," I said. "How's your hem stitch?"

"Oliver, I've sewed up more corpses than you've had hot dinners." He slapped a field dressing on each side of the thigh, and bandaged me with surprising dexterity. "There you are. Good as new."

The engines rumbled into life and we started to move again. "I told Nino to get under way." He hesitated. "What orders, Oliver? How are we going to handle it?"

"God knows," I said. "I'll have to think. Just now all I want to do is sleep."

"I think maybe that's a good idea."

He gave me his hand, but when I stood up I found that I didn't need it, mainly, I think, because the morphine had started to work. Simone came out of the cabin with a tray and I asked her how Wyatt was.

"Not so good," she said. "I think he could do with some sleep."

"Me, too."

I closed the door behind me and climbed on to the spare bunk, tiredness flooding over me. After a while, I turned and found Wyatt watching me, his head on one side, the eyes like dark holes in the gaunt face.

"What a bloody mess," he said.

I nodded weakly. "I'm sorry."

"What happens now?"

"I don't know."

"I'm dying, Grant, you know that, don't you?"

"Perhaps—perhaps not."

He turned and looked up at the ceiling of the cabin. "And Dimitri continues to live." He laughed harshly, choking a little. "Now I don't really see how I can allow that to happen, do you?"

But I hadn't the strength to answer, for suddenly darkness swept over me like the seventh wave and I slept.

CHAPTER FOURTEEN

FACE TO FACE

IT WAS SHORTLY AFTER NOON WHEN I awakened and only then because my leg started to hurt as the effect of the morphine started to wear off. I sat up and found Wyatt's head turned toward me, eyes open. His forehead was pale, almost translucent and damp with sweat.

I said, "Can't you sleep?"

"Rather a waste of time under the circumstances, wouldn't you say?" He smiled faintly. "Do you have any idea what you're going to do yet?"

"Not really."

"Let me know when you do. I'll be happy to go along with anything you decide." He smiled again. "If I'm around long enough, that is."

It was an uncomfortable thought and I got to my feet, opened the door and went into the saloon. There didn't seem to be anybody about, but the medicine chest was on the table. I rummaged about inside until I found the box of morphine ampoules and at that moment Simone came down the companionway.

She was wearing a yellow sou'wester oilskin coat and there was rain on her face which I now saw was quite badly bruised on the right cheek where Langley's elbow had connected.

"So you're up?" she said and then saw the box of ampoules in my hand. "Here, let me do that. How is it?"

"Not so good." I sat down and propped my leg on the table so that she could give me the injection. "What's it like up top?"

"Plenty of rain, winds three to four. Clearing toward evening. I just checked on the radio for Aldo."

"I'll see for myself, I think."

I got to my feet and she protested at once. "You should be taking it easy."

"Some sea air will do me good. I need to clear my head—to think. You have a word with Wyatt. There may be something he needs."

The morphine worked quickly and the pain in the leg was already dying away as I went up the companionway and the rain, stinging my face like lead pellets when I went out on deck, was cold and fresh and made me feel alive again.

Palmyra rolled her slim length into the wind, plunging over a wave as water broke across her prow, racing the weather. On the port side, briefly on the horizon, I seemed to see land, but could not be sure.

In the wheelhouse Barzini leaned over the chart table. Behind him the wheel clicked to one side eerily to compensate as the *Palmyra* veered to starboard, the automatic pilot in control.

"How are you?" he said.

"Fine—crippled, but fine. Where's Nino?"

"Pumping some fuel in the engine room. He'll be along."

I pointed to the horizon. "Did I see land out there?"

"Malta." He tapped the chart. "We should make Capo Passero by early evening if we can maintain speed and the weather doesn't get any worse. I've been pushing her as hard as she'll go."

He took a flask of brandy from the chart table drawer and passed it to me. I took a long swallow and it seemed to explode somewhere deep inside. Probably didn't mix too well with morphine.

I said, "I think we should have a talk, all of us together, to decide what happens at Capo Passero."

"Okay," he said. "She should be all right on automatic pilot for a while. Let's go."

As we went out on deck Nino climbed up from the engine room and Barzini called him to join us as we went below. We sat round the table and Simone brought fresh coffee from the galley.

I said, "All right, Aldo, so we get to Capo Passero. What happens then? You tell me."

"You want your sister. Stavrou wants his stepson. We make a deal."

"But it isn't that simple," I said. "Not anymore. We know now that Stavrou needs his stepson dead. It means a fortune to him. It also means he doesn't want inconvenient witnesses around. Langley was supposed to see to that for him, only he slipped up."

"But Stavrou doesn't know that," Simone put in. "Let's say he comes on the radio like he said he would the moment we're sighted. He'll expect to hear from Langley that Wyatt's dead. That the rest of you have been disposed of."

"So what are you getting at?"

"It's simple. Instead of Langley, he gets you. You tell him Langley was killed during the prison break."

"I see," I said. "He'll have to go through the whole charade as he originally spelled it out."

"That's right. You'll have to have Wyatt on deck as we go in and Stavrou will have Hannah waiting up on the high terrace. You'll go up to the villa, make the exchange."

Barzini shook his head and slammed a hand against the table. "But it isn't meant to be that way. He never intended it to be that way. He wants Wyatt, but he needs him dead. That means he's got to shut our mouths too and money ain't enough, not to a guy like him."

I said to Simone, "What did you think would happen? Originally, I mean?"

"He had to play rough to get you," she said. "I accepted that, but as for the rest," she shrugged. "He sold me the same bill of goods he sold you. Getting Stephen Wyatt out of Râs Kanai was a sacred duty in loving memory of his wife."

"The bastard," Nino said.

"There is one thing in our favor," I said. "The fact that Stavrou doesn't realize how much we know."

"Just a minute," Simone said. "Wouldn't it occur to him that Wyatt would have said rather a lot?"

"That's easy," I shrugged. "I tell him on the radio that Wyatt's badly wounded from the prison break, delirious. No reason he shouldn't accept that."

"So he'll expect you to take Wyatt up to the villa and hand him over in exchange for Hannah and your money."

"Exactly."

"And you'll be ready for anything he tries?"

"Crazy." Barzini slammed his fist against the table. "It doesn't even begin to face the real problem, which is the girl. What happens to her? She's up on the high terrace, right? With that old cow of a woman breathing down her neck. We take Wyatt up there for a confrontation then start a shooting war." He shook his head. "The girl is the first to go."

He was right of course. There was no way round that—no way at all—and then Nino said almost casually, "What we need is someone on the inside."

Simone said, "But that isn't possible. There's no other way up to the villa from the beach except the road."

"Sure there is," Nino said. "There's the cliff."

There was a kind of stunned silence and we all stared at him. "You think you could climb that cliff?" I said incredulously.

"Nothing to it. A goat could get up there. You give me a decent gun, I'll climb up to the high terrace and shoot that old bitch before she has time to lay a glove on your sister."

Barzini clapped an arm about his shoulders and hugged him. "As a Barzini I'm proud of you. When we get back to Palermo I'll buy off the Mafia. This I swear even if you have to marry that damn girl. I don't care what it costs."

It was Simone who put a damper on things. "All very well," she said. "But what about Wyatt? Is capable of going through with all that? Will he want to?"

The cabin door creaked and we turned to find Stephen Wyatt on his feet, leaning in the doorway. He smiled crookedly. "Don't worry about him, Miss Delmas. He wouldn't miss it for anything on top of this earth."

It was still raining as we moved in toward the great cliffs below the villa at Capo Passero. Simone was below with Wyatt, Barzini and I were in the wheel-house, and Nino crouched on the floor out of sight. He wore a wetsuit and aqualung and had a canvas waterproof bag attached to his waist containing climbing boots and a pistol. He had a pair of binoculars out and was busy examining the cliff through a hole Barzini had kicked through a panel for him.

"Like I said, nothing to it," he said. "There's a cleft running all the way up on this side of the point just by the entrance to that bay. I'll go up that way and work my way round to the terrace."

"How long will it take you?"

He had another look through the binoculars. "No more than half an hour. Mind you, I'd better get started, just in case."

"Okay, good luck," I said.

"Go with God," Barzini whispered.

We were perhaps fifty or sixty yards out from the entrance to the bay and Aldo slowed down and swung the wheel, turning *Palmyra* momentarily broadside to the cliffs. Nino pulled down his mask, slid across the deck under the rail and dropped into the sea, going under the surface instantly.

As we turned again toward the entrance to the horseshoe bay, the radio crackled and a voice said, "Come in, *Palmyra!* Come in!" It wasn't Stavrou's.

I picked up the hand mike and flipped the switch. "This is *Palmyra.*"

"Is that you, Mr. Langley?" I recognized the voice then. It was Gatano.

I said, "Langley is dead."

There was a startled exclamation and then Stavrou's voice broke in. "Grant, is that you? What happened?"

"Langley bought it on the way out at Râs Kanai. So did Nino and Angelo Carter."

There was a long pause before he spoke again, his voice harsh and remote. "And my stepson?"

"He's not too good. He was in a bad enough way when we picked him up, then he stopped a bullet. Hasn't been able to say anything that made much sense."

We passed in through the entrance to the bay. The Cessna was still moored to its buoys. He said, "Put Simone on. I want to talk to her."

I looked up at the high terrace. "I don't see my sister, Stavrou."

"You will," he said. "As soon as I see my stepson."

I went below and got Simone and told her what he wanted on the way back. She picked up the mike and said, "Dimitri?"

"What about Justin?"

"Killed," she said. "So were Nino and Angelo, but Dimitri—your son. He's very ill. He needs to get to a hospital as soon as possible."

"I'll take care of that," he said. "First let me see him on deck."

I went below to get Wyatt. He was very pale now, the skin stretched tightly on his face like wrinkled parchment. He wore an old reefer jacket over his prison pajamas.

"How's it going?" he said.

I told him on the way up the companionway and when we went on deck, Barzini came out of the wheelhouse with a folding canvas chair so that he could sit down.

I went back to the radio and picked up the mike. "Satisfied, Stavrou?"

There was a lengthy pause and then he said, "Perfectly."

"And my sister?"

"Look up, sir."

I focussed the binoculars and she jumped into view up there on the top terrace at the iron railings. She was smiling and fondling the Doberman's ears and Frau Kubel was standing close by in the same black bombazine dress.

I picked up the mike, "All right, what now?"

"I'll send the Landrover down. You can all come up and we'll make the exchange. I'll have some really excellent champagne waiting for you. You're a man after my own heart, Major Grant, but then, I had complete confidence in you from the beginning."

I put the mike down and turned to Barzini. "All right, Aldo, take her in and let's get ready."

By the time the Landrover reached the jetty we were ready and waiting, Barzini and I standing on either side of Wyatt, who sat in the canvas chair. We each had an Uzi slung from our right shoulder and I had a Smith and Wesson sticking out of my hip pocket.

The moment the Landrover braked to a halt, Bonetti and Moro jumped out covering us with Sterling sub-machine guns. Gatano got from behind the wheel and came forward.

"What is this?" I demanded.

"No guns!" he said. "Mr. Stavrou's orders."

He took the Uzis and the Smith and Wesson from my pocket and put them in the cab. Which left me with the Stechkin stuck into my belt at the small of my back under my shirt. Barzini had a revolver in the same place and even Simone had a Beretta automatic tucked into the waistband of her slacks under her sweater.

With Moro and Bonetti helping, we manhandled Wyatt into the back of the Landrover still sitting in the canvas chair. He looked really terrible now, his eyes bright and feverish. Once on the brief journey up to the villa I saw him put a hand inside his coat and when he took it out there was blood on the fingers.

We drove in through the entrance to the courtyard and received our first surprise, for Stavrou was standing at the bottom of the steps leading up to the garden, leaning on his canes.

As I got out I looked up and saw Hannah clearly, standing by the railings at the far end of the high terrace, the dog beside her. Frau Kubel was some distance away, leaning over the rail, looking down at what was taking place in the courtyard. There was no sign of Nino.

We lifted Wyatt down in the canvas chair and Barzini and I carried him forward. He kept his chin on his chest and muttered as we put him down, "Get back, you two. I want to talk to him alone. I'll keep it going for as long as I can."

Stavrou tapped his way toward him as Barzini and I moved back to the truck, a genial smile on his face. "Why, Stephen, my boy," he said, "it's good to see you."

Gatano moved to join them and stood on the other side of the chair holding a Sterling. Wyatt raised his head slowly and I saw the dreadful pain on his face, and realized beyond any doubt that he was holding on to the final threads of life with all his strength. And I saw something more—Nino appearing round a buttress, halfway up the wall beneath the far end of the terrace.

Stavrou said something to Wyatt, I don't know what, and Wyatt gave a sudden agonized cry and turned to glance at me over his shoulder. "I'm sorry, Grant, there isn't time."

His hand came out of the right-hand pocket of his reefer coat and he was holding a Sturma stick grenade. There was a moment of total stillness and then, as Stavrou tried to turn, dropping one of his canes, the grenade exploded with devastating effect, taking out Gatano as well.

Barzini had his revolver already in his hand, but it wasn't necessary, for Moro and Bonetti, stunned by what had happened, could only stand and stare at the butcher's shop the courtyard had become.

As for me, I ran for the steps, too late, for high on the terrace, Frau Kubel had turned and was running toward Hannah, gun in hand, and Nino was still just below the overhang.

And then a rather large miracle occurred, for as the old woman paused ten feet away from her target and took careful aim, the Doberman leapt for her throat. She screamed once and they went back together over the rail falling through space, passing from sight to the rocks below.

I kept on going, taking the steps two at a time and arrived on the terrace as Nino scrambled over the rail at the other end. Hannah turned toward me, a hand outstretched.

"Who is it? What's happening?"

"Hannah," I said. "It's me—Oliver."

A look of complete bewilderment appeared on her face and she moved forward, her hands reaching out to touch. And then she smiled.

"Oliver," she said. "What kept you?"

For the first time since childhood I felt like weeping, so intense was the emotion of the moment, but I contented myself with putting my arms around her and holding her as if I'd never let her go.

CHAPTER FIFTEEN

ENDPIECE

WE LEFT AGAIN IN *Palmyra* WITHIN the hour and sailed into Palermo harbor at dawn the following day. I wanted Hannah away from there and back home without delay, so Barzini pulled strings and got us seats on the flight to London that same afternoon.

He took us out to the airport at Punta Raise himself in the yellow Alfa—me, Hannah, and Simone. Nino stayed home, the streets of Palermo still unsafe for him until his uncle had the chance to arrange matters. We had an emotional farewell.

"It was a great climb," I said.

"I know, like the English say, a piece of cake." And then he laughed. "Only in the end it turned out to be a bigger slice than I thought."

At the airport, Barzini and I left the girls talking and moved out on the terrace for a final word. "Well, it was very interesting," he said.

"You can say that again. What do you think the authorities will make of it?"

"Simple enough. With an explosion like that, I'd say they'll assume some of Stavrou's old Mafia pals caught up with him."

"And Moro and Bonetti?"

"They'll button up. No percentage for them in shooting their mouths off." He lit one of his vile Egyptian cheroots. "Yes, it was quite like old times."

"Only we're not as young as we were."

"So you feel that way, too?" He grinned. "Time to settle down, Oliver, with a good woman." He looked inside at Hannah and Simone. "Are you likely to be coming back this way?"

"I don't think so. Not for a while anyway. I need a rest."

"A pity. Still, I'll send her in to you."

He went back to the two girls and after a moment or so of conversation, Simone came out on the terrace.

"Well?" she said.

"Are you all right for money?"

"I have a bank account here. Enough for now. And Aldo's offered me a job, if I want one, doing the stage design at that beach club of his."

"That's nice."

I lit a cigarette. She said, "What will you do? Afterward, I mean?"

"God knows."

She reached out suddenly and touched my hand. "I'm sorry, Oliver."

"What for?"

"You know what I mean. The way things were at the beginning."

"Never apologize for anything," I said. "It's a sign of weakness."

"Damn you!" she said, and then they called our flight over the tannoy and that was very much that.

As for Hannah, I decided to tell her the truth for once in my life, in every detail, and tossed in a few unpleasant facts about her brother while I was at it.

She took it extremely well under the circumstances, which is more than I can say for my grandmother, who received me coldly in the beautiful Victorian drawing room of her house in St. John's Wood and demanded an accounting.

When I was finished she said, "I don't think you should come here again, Oliver. Not for a while at any rate."

"I know," I said. "I'm bad news."

"Bad for Hannah," she replied calmly. "And that is all that concerns me."

Which was fair enough. I stayed in London another two days, mainly to see my lawyer and make certain financial arrangements, then I caught a flight to Madrid where I hired a car and drove south.

It was late afternoon when I arrived at the villa at Cape de Gata. Everything was exactly the same as I had left it on that day a thousand years ago when it had all started—except for one thing. The Alfa was parked in the courtyard.

I had a quick look round the villa, but there was no one there, so I got back into the hired car and drove down toward the marshes.

I found her at the end of the causeway, sitting in front of her easel, painting. When I got out of the car she made no sign. It was, of course, a watercolor as usual, a view of the marsh and the sea and the evening sky beyond, that was very fine indeed.

I said, "You get better all the time. That background wash is fantastic."

She said, "It occurred to me that you wouldn't know where I'd left the Alfa. I thought I'd better return it."

"Thanks," I said.

I lit a cigarette and crouched down beside her. The sea was calm, the evening sky the color of brass. A sandpiper skimmed the water and fled like a departing spirit. It was all very peaceful. I wondered for how long.

CPSIA information can be obtained at www.ICGtesting.com
Printed in the USA
LVOW031005030112

262160LV00001B/78/P

9 781453 200346